Selene's Surrender

~ One Summer in Devon ~

ANGELINA AMOSS

US English has been used throughout.

This is a work of fiction. Names, characters, businesses, places, events and incidents either are the products of the author's imagination or used in a fictitious manner. Any resemblance to actual persons, living or dead, or actual events is purely coincidental.

First Printed Edition, England August 2022

ISBN: 9798845924254

Book cover from Victoria Cooper Art

Index

Index...3
Chapter 1 4
Chapter 2 10
Chapter 3 14
Chapter 4 19
Chapter 5 22
Chapter 6 25
Chapter 7 34
Chapter 8 39
Chapter 9 47
Chapter 10 50
Chapter 11 51
Chapter 12 57
Chapter 13 63
Chapter 14 75
Chapter 15 79
Chapter 16 84
Chapter 17 96
Chapter 18 102
Chapter 19 110
Chapter 20 114
Chapter 21 125
Chapter 22 132
Chapter 23 139
Chapter 24 147
Chapter 25 151
Chapter 26 159
Chapter 27 164
Chapter 28 173
Chapter 29 181
Chapter 30 191
Chapter 31 196
Chapter 32 200
Chapter 33 208
Chapter 34 220
Chapter 35 227
Chapter 36 233
Chapter 37 240
Epilogue 243

Chapter 1

Selene – Ultimate Rejection

I SHOULD BE DEVASTATED, HEARTBROKEN. But I'm not. I'm livid, furious, and a *great* deal relieved. Mark had been the boy next door, until we married and moved into a very respectable stylish new build detached in Northwich. Four bedrooms no less, what a waste of space that turned out to be. I had my mother's dream wedding – I'd wanted a small affair, but no one listened. Big white dress, a hundred people, half of whom I didn't know and I don't believe I've ever met again.

Tall, slim, handsome, Mark was the catch every girl I knew wanted. And he chose me, wow, how unlucky was I!

I never understood why he picked me. I knew he wasn't right for me, you know… all the too's. Too good-looking, rich, intelligent, sporty, generous, and way too good to be true!

I should have listened to my instincts.

But mum talked me round. Told me I was beautiful and kind, and that Mark and I went together like a horse and carriage – well she didn't say that, but I thought it. Mark the stallion and me the sturdy reliable carriage, going wherever I was led.

When mum died of a brain tumor a year ago, it had been Mark's parents that consoled me. Mark did all the obvious things, flowers, cuddles, special words on cards, texts and even emails when his job took him overseas just three weeks after mum's funeral. But Kevin and Judith had been the ones who understood, who held me tight and said nothing. Who passed me cups of tea without asking if I wanted one. They'd guided me through all the nightmares of taking care of someone's estate – like mum had lived in a mansion or something.

We sold mum's comfortable home of thirty years, it broke my heart but it only reminded me of my parents who were now both gone. At the time Mark told me I should keep it, maybe rent it out. Of course *now* I know why, because if I'd listened to him I wouldn't be homeless right now.

It's a funny thing being loaded, but at the same time having nowhere to live. The word disembodied keeps crossing my mind. I have this image of my limbs breaking away from my body and floating through the air. You see I've been pulled apart, broken into pieces. I can't imagine ever being whole again.

Right now I'm staying in Shelley's spare bedroom in her swanky flat in Manchester. Marvelous friend that she is, I can't intrude for long. I am sort of uncomfortable, lost, and out of sync. The trouble is I don't know what I want to do with the rest of my life.

When mum got ill I gave up work to look after her, when she died I just somehow never ended up going back into the rat race. It felt meaningless. I know I'd rather be a hobo, than get on a train one more time and travel to my old job in Manchester. Just the thought of it still causes my throat to constrict and my heart to flip-flop. I was an excellent accountant, but it brought me not one iota of joy or satisfaction.

Don't get me wrong. I'm not lazy or anything. I work like a Trojan once I find something I want to do. Mark said I'm an all or nothing kind of person. Which is funny because... once he'd wanted all of me, now he wants none of me!

No, no, I mustn't exaggerate. He's kind. He's upset that he's hurt me. Knowing me well, he understands I've been set adrift without an anchor.

God knows where I'll end up.

That's the problem isn't it? Hating someone who is kind and hard to fault, it makes confusion run riot. I'm not confused though, I *do* hate him. Not for finally admitting he's gay, but for robbing me of the last twelve years of my life. Oh my days, for that I *really* hate him.

We can't get back our youth can we? We can't slip back into that size ten dress now that we've drifted into a fourteen. Can't erase the early stages of lines, not without surgery anyway, and that route I'm never taking. I mean have you seen some celeb faces? One singer in particular can't even smile anymore. Exceptional singer though! Love her songs. Just wish she'd left her face alone.

I want to go on social media and scream to the world – do you know what this *beep-beep* man has done to me? But mum had thirty odd years to ingrain in me the way a lady should behave, and washing your dirty laundry in public is something any *lady* with *pride* should *never* do. So, although she is dearly departed from the world, she still remains inside me refusing to leave. I've hit the wine until

I'm staggering around like a jelly baby, but even that doesn't shut her up.

And so I ramble… because I'm lost, and thinking about someone else is easier than focusing on myself.

I thought I knew where my life was going, thought I knew who I was.

Jeez, but I hate change, more, I must say, than I hate Mark.

The irritating thing is, I know in a short while I'll forgive him, because we're both basically solid, kind people, and I hate to hate, it makes me ill.

'LIFE'S A BITCH, but you just got to attack it head on.'

I roll my eyes, I can't help it. Shelley is so dramatic and bombastic. She's also very often right. 'I can't face looking for a job just yet. There's this crazy tornado firing up inside me, and if I keep squashing it down and don't deal with it, I'm going to explode.'

'Alright then, what are you going to do?'

'Trying to get rid of me?'

She chucks a cushion at me. 'Don't be daft.'

'I was thinking of taking a holiday.'

'*Now* you're talking. Where are you going to go? I know, Paris to take up art and a passionate lover.'

I laugh, but shake my head.

'Oh, oh, I know, New York where all the hip people are. You can go all metropolitan and mingle with a hive of people rushing to enjoy life.'

One eyebrow rises, 'Absolutely not.'

'OK, how about LA? You can mingle with the stars and your next lover can be a famous actor.'

I shake my head. 'You were half-way there with Paris.'

'I give in, where you thinking?'

'Devon.'

'What?' Shelley nearly falls off the sofa. 'I don't mean to be rude Selene, but you've got a shit pile of money, why on earth do you want to go to Devon?'

'I want some peace and quiet.' I can't help laughing at Shelley's pulled face. 'You'll think me nuts I know, but I want to take up painting again.'

'You do?'

'Yes. I've been doing some research. I'm going to do an on-line course. It's pretty basic but I need to start somewhere. I did art at school, but that was donkey's years ago. This is a three-month course, soooo,' dramatic pause, 'I thought I'd hire a cottage and go and live in Devon while I do it.'

'You know you could go anywhere in the world? If I was you, I'd be off to Bali or somewhere exotic like that, lounge on the beach, drink cocktails, get a suntan, have a fling, live a little.'

'Yes, but I'm not you.'

'But…'

I tilt my head and fix her with a stare.

'OMG! I'm sorry. I'm not trying to be pushy; I just want you to have some fun that's all.'

'Who says I won't have fun in Cockington?'

Chapter 2

Giovanni – Living the Dream

STANDING ON THE BALCONY I gaze down at St James's Square, a tiny piece of green in the middle of London, the place to be and be seen. My bachelor pad set me back fifteen million, but it's worth it. It's the height of comfort in one of the most vibrant cities in the world. I wouldn't want to be anywhere else.

'Gio, honey, is it OK if I grab a shower?'

'Help yourself.'

I check out Coco as she strolls across the living room towards the guest suite. She's stunning, tall, slender, and has fab slightly-slanted brown eyes that you want to dive into. She's got an ace personality too, makes me laugh so much, which is unusual for an escort. She's also incredibly loyal and discrete about her clients. Which is why I hire her often, when I'm in-between my various flings. No pressure, just lots of fun.

I love my lifestyle, my famiglia not so much! Poor momma will have no knuckles left, if she keeps biting them every time she sees me.

London is where head office is, I tell her, when she begs me with pleading praying-positioned hands to move to Devon. I won't tell you her response, but it does include a few choice Italian words.

I love Torquay, where nearly all the family live now, but London makes me tick. I love the fast pace and luxurious lifestyle, and hey who wouldn't enjoy the clubs, and the girls that throw themselves at designer suits?

'Espresso?' I call out as I make my way across to the kitchen.

'Please, honey.'

Love the smell of strong coffee; sure the caffeine hits me before I've even had a sip.

Just as I'm knocking back the strong, black liquid, my phone starts vibrating. Only family would call me this early on a Sunday morning. I pick it up and swipe straight away.

'Ciao, Lorenzo, what's up?'

'Gio, it's Nonna, she's had a fall and is in hospital, I thought you'd want to know.'

My heart rate quickens. 'Is she alright?' Silly question, obviously when a seventy-eight-year-old woman has a fall, she's not going to be OK.

'Yes, yes, don't worry. She's had an x-ray and nothing's broken, they're letting us take her home shortly, but she's going to need someone with her full time until she's back on her feet…'

I cut in. 'I'm coming.' I look at my watch, fifteen minutes to get ready, four hours in the car. 'I'll be with you about noon.'

'Are you sure? I know you're busy. I only phoned to let you know, keep you in the loop.'

'I want to be there.' Grandfather died last year, and Papà had a heart attack ten months ago, he pulled through OK, and has changed his lifestyle after his warning. But all of a sudden, life seems more precious. Who knows how much more time I've got left with Nonna?

'OK, well drive carefully. See you later.'

'Yep, and thanks for calling.'

Before I can even ask Coco to leave she appears, bag over her arm. She saunters over and places a friendly kiss on my cheek. 'Drive slowly,' she warns me.

'Thanks babe, will do.' Of course I don't keep to speed limits, but it's just easier to tell everyone that I do.

As soon as the door closes I send a text to Catherine, my housemaid. I ask her to come tomorrow for a 'full' clean. She understands what that means. I've got just a touch of OCD, I mostly have it under control and I seriously don't see the problem with keeping everything perfectly straight… and very clean. But after visitors, well let's just say thank God for Catherine, because she knows exactly what I want, and after company, that's a spring-clean from top to bottom. She'll come with her two girls and by the end of the day not a speck of dust will be anywhere – especially the bedroom.

The underground car park is a cold concrete box, but it keeps the Lamborghini safe and clean. Jim, the car park attendant, raises a hand to acknowledge me. The whole place is security wired, and technology-proofed to prevent theft, so Jim is basically here to wash our cars and keep the car park spotless.

I like him a lot; he's cheerful and somehow always has the latest celebrity gossip. How he finds out stuff before the newspapers print it is beyond me. If I ever move I'm determined to take him with me. I gave him a tip to buy some shares last year, and I know he made a pretty penny on them. He's looked after me, and most importantly Sherry (my Lamborghini) ever since.

Driving out of London is a nightmare, but I'm used to it. At least it's not raining, in fact it's been very dry and warm this year, which is causing a problem for England's farming. By the time I hit the motorway, the June sun is blaring. After turning on the air conditioning, I press play on my Spotify playlist. Vivaldi, Verdi and Puccini are on a mix so I don't know what's coming next. I turn the volume up; it's a long drive to Cockington.

Chapter 3

Selene – Someone I Used to Know

THE CABRIOLET SOFT-TOP IS BACK. My hair's tied back. And as I drive, I'm singing at full-belt. Lung's wide, spirit soaring. Freedom fuels the power of the words as I sing along with Gotye...

> *Now and then I think of when we were together*
> *Like when you said you felt so happy you could die*
> *Told myself that you were right for me*
> *But felt so lonely in your company*
> *But that was love and it's an ache I still remember*
> *(Gotye 2011)*

I've left Mark a letter, nothing like ink on paper for letting the real you out into the open. Thank you, that's how I'd started my grievance.

> *Dear Mark*
>
> *Thank you. My life would have been different if I hadn't met you, and although maybe in hindsight I should never have said yes, I am glad to have been Mrs. Hastings for a while. For your kindness during mum's illness, thank you. For allowing me to call Kevin and Judith parents for a while, thank*

you. For always picking up after yourself and for never moaning when I didn't fancy cooking – thank you.

For the very generous settlement offer and for finally manning up (ha-ha) to your secret desires, seriously, thank you. Better late than never! And I'm legitimately trying to believe that!

But... and there's always a 'but' isn't there? I'm struggling to release the anger I have over the years you've stolen from me, the time when I could have found someone who loved me, wanted me... desired me. I'm struggling with how unattractive I felt because of all the times you rejected me. I'm trying to be magnanimous, I am, but there's a burning heat in my chest that wants to explode. You stole from me. My youth, my innocence, and my faith in the world that what you see is what you get – boy is that a lie!

I feel jaded, tarnished. A fool and a victim. I know you're not a bad man, and that you did what you thought you had to. But you've stolen from me! I've been robbed.

I'm sorry to unburden on you via letter, but I'm just not able to say what I really think out loud. I realize I have some sort of 'conditioning' problem, that's on me, not you. My emotional wiring is all wrong. I guess when you rejected me in the bedroom I should have demanded to know why, to yell at you until you told me the truth. Instead, I conformed. Became the dutiful wife, smiled and pretended it was alright, hey, it's not your fault if I'm so unattractive. What a lie!

I don't ever want to be that person again!

I'm leaving in search of a new life, a new me. I guess not having me on your doorstep will enable you and Justin to move ahead with your lives.

Be happy Mark and make sure my pain is remembered, so you don't ever do this again.

With as much willpower as I can muster, I forgive you.

Now the… 'Ex'

Selene xx

Why two kisses I have no idea. I'd rather hit him over the head with a hammer than ever kiss him again, but hey-ho, that's how I always sign off, and I find it nearly impossible to break habits.

Oh, the words of this song kill me…

But felt so lonely in your company
But that was love and it's an ache I still remember

I'm not going to cry, I'm not going to cry, I'm not going to cry.

The threatening tears subside. All my life I have conformed. I've done my best to fit in and to make everyone around me happy, at the expense of losing myself. I've reached a point where I literally have *no* idea who I am anymore.

Think positive. Think positive. Think positive.

I *will* discover what it is that makes me tick.

No more pushy mother talking me into doing things I don't want to. I will squash her nagging voice, God bless her, but that has got to go.

No more bosses telling me I'm brilliant and that I've *got* to proceed.

No more gay-husband suppressing me in a box of frustrated emotions.

I *will* learn how to say yes and no in the place where I want to say them, and not where I feel obliged to say them.

Excitement and anxiety bounce in my stomach, holding hands and playing skipping games.

This is the first time I've ever chosen a holiday destination myself.

This is the first time in my life that I'm going to be living on my own, and at thirty-three I think this is long overdue.

My phone rings, I press answer on the hands-free.

'How you doing?'

'For goodness' sake Shelley, I only left you two hours ago!'

'I know, but I just wanted to check you're doing OK. You know you can turn around and come back if you want.'

'Thanks, but no thanks. I'm really looking forward to this. I'm on the precipice of an adventure, thrilled and excited.'

'Umm.'

'Don't worry about me. I'm going to be fine, and I'm still in England, so I can get in the car and drive back to yours in Manchester whenever I want.'

'Too right you can! Whenever you want, I'm here for you. Please don't think that you've got nowhere to go, promise me.'

'I promise, now bugger off so I can go back to singing my head off.'

Shelley laughs, and that encourages me.

'Bye then, have fun you crazy lady.'

The June sun is shining down on me as I speed along the M6 traveling south, to a whole new world, and hopefully a whole new me.

Chapter 4

Giovanni – Damn, What Legs!

SERVICE STATIONS ARE MY kind of hell, I hate stopping at them and prefer to drive right through, but nature's calling. I indicate and pull off at Bridgwater Services. I'll do a quick in and out, and grab a coffee to go.

It's fairly quiet, thank goodness. I drive to the far end of the car park and deliberately park over the line to stop anyone parking next to me. Scratches give me a heart attack, as far as possible I take no chances. Just as I'm opening the door, a red Cabriolet pulls in on the right, also going over the line so that the parking lot between us is now tiny. I glance over to see who's driving as I click the fob to lock. I do a double-take. I'd been expecting a guy, someone my age maybe. What I see instead is a stunning red-head.

She nods to acknowledge my smile, but doesn't return it. Instead, she's out the car and charging towards the facilities on a double-march. I grin; she's clearly stopped for the same reason as me.

I walk behind her, at a more leisurely pace. She's wearing shorts, giving me a view I like a lot. Damn, what legs! Long, slender but curvy in the right places. I'm such a leg-man, they kind of *'do it'* for me. I can image running my hands up and down them, or better still my tongue. My glance travels up her body. I would take a guess that she's a size twelve or fourteen; she's curvaceous in all the right places, that's why her legs are so sexy. She's a long way off the type of women I normally date who somehow all think they need to be thin as a rake, with blown up lips and crazy eyebrows.

Bathroom visited and hands washed for exactly three minutes, I make my way to the coffee bar. Another shot of strong caffeine is called for. As I'm leaving with my own travel cup topped up, I notice the redhead again. Wow, but she's a stunner. If I wasn't in a rush to see Nonna, I'd definitely stop and chat her up.

I look over the red Cabriolet before I get back in Sherry. It's a year old, pretty cool car. I wonder what she does for a living to be able to afford it, she's probably got it on lease, I think as I head off again.

Fifteen minutes away from home, I give Sofia a call.

'Ciao Bella, are you with Nonna?'

'Hey you, yep we're all here. The stubborn mule is at Willows, she refuses to come home with us. We're going to have to take it in turn to stay with her.'

'I've sent a message into the office telling them I'm working from home. I'll stay with Nonna for the first few days.'

'Momma said you would say that,' laughs Sofia. 'You're too predictable Gio.'

'Do you want me to change?'

'Yes!' she laughs, 'we all do. Give up being a gigolo and settle down already.'

'I keep telling you, nobody wants me.'

'How long until you arrive?'

'About ten minutes now, see you soon.'

Chapter 5

Selene – Heaven on Earth

COCKINGTON TAKES MY BREATH AWAY. It's the most quintessential English village I've ever seen. The photographs on the web don't do it justice. I'm as giddy as a child on Christmas Eve.

'Lord, I think I'm in Heaven, thank you.' My eyes have misted up. I blink to knock them away. I can't cry now I'm still driving. The instructions to the holiday let are easy to follow and I'm pulling into a drive just a small stretch away from the tiny village.

A traditionally built stone wall encases the property. As it curves onto the drive, a metal plate states 'Willows' in curvy writing. On the left, there's a large more modern-styled white-washed house. To the right a cottage that belongs in a fairy tale. I drive passed the white house as instructed and follow the cobbled driveway around the back. Another traditional stone cottage, with a low-hanging thatch roof is in front of me. I recognize it from the web's photos, it's perfect and I think I'm so excited my head is going to burst. Blood in the Cabriolet not a pleasant image, I take a deep breath.

As I step out of the car I'm in awe of the silence of everything except nature: leaves rustling in the light breeze, birds tweeting all around. I can't hear traffic; I think I've arrived at Heaven on Earth. I love that the door is unlocked, and that my key waits for me on the kitchen table. I would never have dreamed of leaving my door unlocked back home.

Wow, with an outside that resembles a Constable painting, I wasn't expecting it to be quite so modern inside. I know from the description given that it's a four-roomed house: an open kitchen living room, two bedrooms and a bathroom. I thought it might be dark, how wrong could I be? To the left of the door are two sofas sitting opposite each other with a wooden coffee table between them. The table is on black wheels and I know straight away that it's been made from an old railway sleeper, it's quirky and I love it. To the right is the kitchen, modern and chrome. The walls are white and reflect the light from the small kitchen window and the large patio doors which sit in the wall adjacent the sofas.

I step outside. A series of square white stone pillars hold a series of six-foot wooden panels. There's a round glass table, two chairs and a bench. The area is tiny and has been stone-flagged. Bamboo grows in several terracotta pots. It's small but stylish. Whoever put this place together has a talent for decorating.

Back inside I check the fridge and an 'aww' escapes me. Inside are the essentials, including eggs, butter and cheese, and a pile of salad items. On the kitchen counter are a farmhouse loaf and a bottle of red wine. A little note propped against the wine says – Enjoy your holiday xx. How sweet is that?

I go back to the car and start the task of unloading. I've brought quite a lot with me. Besides clothes and toiletries, I've purchased piles of painting equipment including two easels, one stand-up to stay in the cottage, and another which folds down into a case, for taking with me on days out – should I get brave enough to paint in public that is.

After unpacking, I send Shelley a quick text to let her know I arrived safely.

It's only three o'clock and all of a sudden I'm disorientated. A ship on land, a bird with clipped wings, something causes my world to tilt, trying to cast me off. What should I do? I don't want to start the art course after such an early start, and it's Sunday after all. The walls close in on me, and then slide out again. I shoot a hand out and hold the back of the sofa to steady myself.

Blood is pounding in my ears. What have I done? Am I crazy?

By fleeing Cheshire all I've done is trapped myself in limbo, purgatory of unwanted wives. Why did I think Devon would be my salvation?

I've pinned all my hopes on these twelve weeks. What if I've made a mistake? I need to get out.

After freshening up, I change into a dress and head out.

I decide to go for a drive and explore the area. I also resolve to have my first meal out. I won't plan it, I'll just drive until I find somewhere I fancy stopping. Spontaneous – the new me!

Chapter 6

Giovanni – Something about Her

I STOPPED BEING EXCITED about scantily dressed bunnies a long time ago. Now, I appreciate the more seductive soft flows of clothes that hide but promise. I like undressing with my eyes, way before I reach to undo buttons. There's something infinitely sexy about a woman who is completely unaware of her appeal. And I'll admit I get a kick out of the chase. The harder she ignores my efforts – the more I want her.

I'm not proud that once the conquest is acquired I quickly lose interest, but it's just who I am. To date (and I'm thirty-eight) I've only had one significant other. Jojo. Still have mixed thoughts about her, I mean she's hot, like damn hot. She put up with me for eighteen months – I mean geez, Momma was planning the wedding. Not Nonna, she didn't approve at all, but the rest of the family was picking out wedding presents.

I shudder.

Scary stuff, very near miss… but then again did I mention she's hot? She's a Vogue model and a drop-dead stunner. Long black hair, super sexy long legs… (albeit too thin) and as you know, I'm a leg man through and through. She parties hard and we'd had crazy wild sex, we totally got each other in the bedroom. The trouble for me was that the bedroom was the only place we really got each other. She's smart and very career minded, which I admire a lot, but we just didn't have things to talk about. My friends thought I was crazy when I finally called an end to it.

Click, click.

I startle and look up.

John's snapping his fingers at me. 'Where you at, Bud?'

I laugh, 'Far away.'

'No shit. Come on we're going back to Danni's for a few beers around the fire pit.'

I look across the room; she's still there – the flaming-haired vision that just sent me off into my internal reverie. From the moment she'd walked into the restaurant I could think of nothing else but undressing her. I'd been throwing glances her way for the last half hour, but haven't been able to catch her eye.

She's reading a book while halfheartedly eating mouthfuls of risotto. Seriously, how can she not be giving that rice her full attention? It's momma's finest recipe. People normally moan when they first taste it, and there she is shoving another fork full in and not even looking at it!

'Hey, Gio, come on snap out of it. Let's go.'

I stand and chuck a thumb's up at Pierre, he'll add our bill to my tab. Papà lets me and my friends eat at half price, but never for free. Business is business after all, and we may own the restaurant, but we've left the management to Pierre and his staff for years now.

My feet are carrying me, but I don't want to leave.

Danni is tapping her foot by the door. 'Hey slow-coaches, let's get moving!' Her lyrical but loud voice causes my redhead to finally look up. I'm waiting. Eye's lock. I smile.

Her face doesn't move. Come on woman, acknowledge, I stretch the grin as far as it will go, just so she's clear I'm smiling at her. There! She half-laughs before returning to her book. What a fire-cracker, mio Dio let her be here long term and not for a one-week holiday.

My feet have taken root outside the restaurant door.

'Are you coming?' Danni calls from the side of her car.

Sofia is with Nonna and I told her I wouldn't be long, although she told me to stay out all night if I wanted. But I don't want to.

'Hey guys, I'm going to call it a night. I want to be with Nonna, and I've got a pile of emails that need sending.'

'No problem, Bud, great to see you again, and thanks again for dinner.'

'No problem.' And it isn't. The tab is small-fry to me, but to my friends I know it stretches their budget. 'Are we surfing this weekend?'

'What do you think?'

I laugh. Of course we are. 'Where we going?'

'We're meeting up with the others at Bantham Beach at six, you coming?'

'Absolutely, see you there.'

I wave them off and head towards Sherry, but as I reach for the handle an image of a certain red-head floats before me. I turn around and go back.

'HI.' IT'S THE MOST underestimated word in the dictionary. Depending on tone and setting and the person receiving, the short word can mean a hundred different things. My tone is low. I try for husky. She knows it's a word just for her. I convey – hi, I think you're sexy, do you mind if I take you to bed? What other word could carry such a meaning?

'Hi.'

I want to laugh. That 'hi' was short and sharp, it conveyed – hi, bugger off you're interrupting and I want to be left alone. See, it can mean a hundred different things that one little word.

'Do you mind?' I point at the chair opposite her.

'Actually, I'm enjoying my space, so…'

I cut in on my little firecracker, 'I won't take long, I would just like to introduce myself and chat, five minutes max, what do you say?'

She glances around. People are curious and looking our way. Her face pings pink. Advantage me, but I won't sit until she says. She gives the briefest of nods, while sitting back in her chair, an obvious attempt to put the biggest distance between us.

I sit. I give myself two minutes to unwind her coiled antagonism, and then the hunt can commence full steam ahead.

'Thanks, I won't keep you long I promise. But I just couldn't leave without taking the time to meet you. You're stunning, if you don't mind me saying.'

Her lips purse tight together, oh she's one of *those*. Doesn't believe she's attractive and can't stand compliments. I'll have to remedy that.

'You don't believe, but trust me, you're bellissima.' I'm in sultry level mode and upped the heavy Italian accent, chicks love it. I'm also keeping eye contact. She keeps glancing down; she doesn't know where to look. Oh, momma mia, I'm going to enjoy this.

'I'm Giovanni,' I offer my hand.

She accepts it. I fold my fingers around her hand and pull it towards my mouth before she can resist. Keeping my eyes locked on hers, I plant a kiss on the back of her hand. Usually, I would turn it over and kiss the palm, much more intimate, but she's throwing off vibes of wanting to flee, so I resist.

'Selene,' she snaps, snatching back her hand and putting it on her lap, out of my reach.

'What brings you to Torquay?' Please don't say holiday.

She closes her book. I can see by her demeanor that's she's trying to work out what to tell me, speak the truth Bella. I hate liars.

She sighs, giving in, and I'm over the first hurdle. 'I'm on an extended holiday.'

I can't help smiling, I've got more than a week then.

'How do you like the English Riviera so far?'

'I just arrived today actually, but what I've seen so far I love.' She's smiling, reflecting the truth in her words. Damn, but she's a Goddess when she smiles.

'I know, we met earlier today.'

'We did?' She seems confused.

I lose myself in her gold and forest-green eyes. There is a kind of viridian green that speaks to the soul of nature, of fresh blades of grass and dark forest secrets. Her eyes are that bright color, bold and beautiful.

Something sparks inside me, I catch my breath. 'Wow, your eyes are something else!'

A tiny half smile curves her luscious, perfectly shaped lips, and I want to kiss them – really badly. I pull myself together.

'At the services, you pulled in next to me.'

Her eyes drift to the left as she pulls on her memory.

'Oh! Mr. Silver Lamborghini.'

'That's me.' I'm more than a bit miffed that she didn't instantly recognize me, but remembers Sherry!

'How do you plan to fill your days?'

She fidgets. Her Spanish-style, off the shoulder dress rustles. Oh, but I'd like to run my finger under that frill and lower the dress even more. *My friend* flicks and stirs in my jeans. I want to take her in my arms and crush her lips against mine, I want… 'Sorry, what did you say?'

'I said… I'm going to do an online art course and catch up on my reading.' The little spark I'd managed to draw out of her a moment ago has faded. *Idioto!* I could almost bite my knuckle for losing my concentration. Now I've got to peddle quickly, before I lose her altogether.

'When you're not doing those things, could I show you around? I know some fun things we can do that are a bit off the beaten track.'

'That's kind of you…'

I cut in, 'One afternoon, if you don't enjoy yourself I promise to disappear from your life for good. Poof!' I kiss the tips of my fingers then flick them in the air between us.

'Do you always do that?'

Ouch, sharp tone. I shrug. 'Do what?'

'Cut people off when they're in a middle of a sentence.'

Momma mia! But she's tetchy; oh this is going to be so much fun! 'Only when I think a beautiful woman is about to turn me down. Please say yes, Bella, just one afternoon?'

Her brow furrows, she chews her bottom lip. Nearly there, wait for it… wait for it…

'OK then.'

Hook, line and sinker! I grin. 'Fabulous, can we swap numbers?'

She hesitates, but I'm reeling her in. 'I promise I'm not an axe murderer or anything. In fact, my family owns this

31

restaurant, so if you want a reference we can ask the manager. Pierre!' I wave at him.

Selene is blushing. I didn't even know women did that anymore, not like bright red tomatoes anyway.

'Please don't,' she hisses.

So my firecracker doesn't like any sort of attention, I wonder what's caused that?

I shake my head at Pierre and he turns back to the desk.

'You really own this place?'

I'm about to burst out my usual boast about owning half of Torquay, but stop myself. I have the distinct impression money doesn't impress her. 'My parents do, but they've sort of semi-retired now, so Pierre runs it for them.'

I know the next question out of her mouth will be to ask me what I do. Before that can happen I ask, 'Can I have your phone? I'll pop my number into it, and then it will be completely up to you if we meet again. If I don't hear from you, I'll know you want to be left on your own.'

She opens her bag, and passes me her phone after unlocking it. I take it and type my name and number into her contacts, and then pass it back.

Time to go. I stand. She looks slightly surprised. Ha! But I'm the best at this game. I offer my hand, which she accepts hesitantly. I bring it to my lips and place the briefest kiss upon it.

She doesn't take her eyes off me.

And just like that, I know she'll be in my sheets within a week. Damn but I'm good.

Back in the car, I sit there for a moment. All I can think about is how her eyes drew me in, and how much I wanted to undress her, but beyond those two things there's something about her I can't quite put my finger on.

I glance at myself in the mirror, 'Just for fun Gio, just for fun.' But even as I say the words I can hear the hollowness of them. I think I'm going to have to be careful around her, I'm a sworn bachelor and even the most beautiful eyes in the world aren't going to change that.

Chapter 7

Selene – To Text or not to Text

HOW DO YOU DESCRIBE eyes that pull you in and absorb your soul?

'They're brown, but flecked with red and oozing life. I don't know how to describe them, the best way is probably to say that they're one hundred per cent come-to-bed eyes.'

Shelley roars. I'm not so sure what she finds funny. 'And there was me thinking you wouldn't see much action in Devon!'

'I've not seen any action, and I don't intend to either. He just gave me his number that's all, I haven't even decided if I'm going to text him yet.'

'Tall, dark, handsome, a proper Italian Stallion, oh-my-God Selene, you've got to text him!'

I'm beginning to wish I hadn't mentioned him. 'So, do you have a busy week planned?'

'My weekly plan is as dull as dishwater. Let's talk about yours.'

I groan, she giggles.

'OK, we'll stop talking about the drop-dead-gorgeous fella that chatted you up… for now. Tell me what you're going to do today.'

'I need to go grocery shopping, fill the fridge, get some bits and pieces, then this afternoon I want to go to the beach somewhere, feel the sand between my toes.'

'I wish I could take a week off and come and be with you, we'd have so much fun.'

This holiday isn't about fun for me, it's for learning about myself and trying to figure out what direction my future should take, but, a couple of days with giddy Shelley would be fun. 'You could always try and get a Friday off work and just come down for the weekend. Not this coming weekend though,' I rush to add, I want to unwind on my own first.

'Oh yeah, fab idea. I'll check with work and see if there are any available Fridays I can pick. I'll call you when I know. Talking of work, I best get moving, be no good turning up late if I'm going to ask for an unplanned holiday!'

'See ya, have a nice day.'

'You too… and text the stallion!'

I laugh, 'Maybe.'

Before I go out, I decide to Google the restaurant I was at last night, do some fishing and see what I can learn about Giovanni. The restaurant's called *Da Casa a Casa*, which when I put it through the translator I learn means – home from home. What a lovely name. I discover it's owned by the Giacomelli family. I zoom in on a family photograph on the restaurant's website. It looks like grandparents, parents and four siblings. Giovanni's there, but the photo must have been taken a while ago because he appears much younger. I save the image, deciding to send it to Shelley later.

After popping on a summer dress and flip-flops, I drive into town for a leisurely stroll and exploration. I drop bags off in the trunk of the car with lots of salads and cold cut meats. This week I want to just switch off and work as little as possible, so I plan lots of salads and eating out once a day, even if it's just for cappuccino and cake.

The sea breeze is exhilarating, and a walk along the beach with sand on my bare feet thrills me. The summer holidays haven't started yet, and as its Monday, the beach is fairly empty. White fluffy clouds are speeding across a cornflower blue sky. The sea spray is salty and the air fresh. I wish I'd brought my costume so I could go for a swim. Next time, I tell myself.

I find a café along the seafront and take a seat outside after ordering coffee and a cream scone. Very fattening, but I'm in Devon after all! I take pictures of the beach and the scone, and send them to Shelley.

A text comes back straight away: *Great pics, have you texted?*

I send her a laughing face emoji.

I pull up his name, he didn't write Giovanni, he'd simply put Gio, like we'd been friends for ages.

I didn't have any intention of texting him when he wrote his number in my phone last night, but now I'm staring at his number the urge to text is strong.

Here's the dilemma: I'm here to learn about me and to start making right decisions, so with that in mind I shouldn't text. On the other hand he's probably the most strikingly handsome man I've ever met. His hair is short, black and curly. His eyebrows thick and black, his eyes… sigh. His lips are full and very kissable, utterly tempting. And, the clincher for me – his pert, perfectly shaped butt, like two hard footballs. Something about a firm, nicely round bottom excites me, and as Gio walked out of the restaurant last night it was all I could look at. Clearly, he works out.

For just a moment the image of being swooped up in his strong arms and being carried to bed fills me. Heat pours into my cheeks. I close my eyes and imagine his strong thighs, naked, pinning me down.

My eyes shoot open. Gosh, that's not like me! I've never had fantasies in my life. I put the phone away quick.

After the delicious scone and coffee I had back to the car. In the driving seat, I pull out my phone and unlock it.

I can't stop thinking about him.

I press send: *Hi, this is Selene.*

I can see by the flashing icon that he's responding straight away: *Hi, thanks for the text. Can I take you out for dinner?*

Me: *You said afternoon.*

Gio: Thumbs up emoji: *I did. Can we meet tomorrow at 2?*

Me: *Sure.*

Gio: *Fab, I'll send you the address later, just in a meeting.*

He's texting me while he's in a meeting? I would have got sacked if I'd used my phone whilst in a meeting.

Me: *OK.*

Gio: *Ciao Bella x*

I don't reply.

Well I haven't even been here twenty-four hours yet, and I can confidently say I'm changing already! Go me!

Chapter 8

Giovanni – A Fun Date

I'M GOING TO HAVE TO move around some Zoom appointments, but it should be easy. I'll get my secretary Kevin, onto it. As soon as Selene's text came through I got a buzz. There's something about her that excites the pants off me.

A fun afternoon, which I'll do my best to stretch into dinner, is what's needed. I'm going to show her such a wonderful time, she'll forget all about clock watching. But what should we do for a first date?

Most dates I've had have gone straight to wine-and-dine and clubs, that's mostly all the women seem to want anyway. Selene, umm, I somehow don't think she fits into the normal mold, she's definitely no bunny anyway, and I don't think she has a clue as to who my family are. So many times I've seen the look in women's eyes change when they realize I'm worth billions. If I can, I'd like to keep that look out of Selene's eyes. It would be fun to just let her believe we own a few restaurants and not a company ranked ninety-two in the Top 500 Fortune List.

I'm a bit of a workaholic, normally in the office by six-thirty in the morning, and often there until nine at night. I rarely take a holiday, which is one of the reasons my dates don't become long term, they're too needy and get pouty when I don't spend time with them. I guess that's one of the reasons Jojo and I hit it off so well, because her work ethic is up there with mine.

Nonna's housekeeper comes into the office. 'Can I get anything for you Mr. Giacomelli? It's gone two; could I bring you a light lunch?'

I glance at my watch. Where has the day gone? 'Has Nonna gone for a rest?'

'Yes sir, she's just gone to bed.'

'And you're staying until four?'

'Yes, but I can stay later if you need me.'

'No, that's OK Teresa; I'll be back before four. I just want to go and see Papà for a quick meeting.'

'No problem, I won't leave until you're back. Mrs. Giacomelli has requested minestrone for dinner, she doesn't want any other courses, if you let me know what you would like I can prepare it for you?'

'Are you making your focaccia to go with it?'

She smiles. 'Yes sir. The Greek basil is ready to pick, with garlic and a drop of olive oil it will be just how you like it.'

'Splendid, I look forward to it. No need to do anything else that will be enough for me, grazie Teresa.'

As I drive over to the family home and see the sun glistening on the waves it inspires my first idea for tomorrow's date.

Parked up, I pull out my mobile and send Selene a text. I give her the address and tell her to come in beachwear.

I laugh at her economic reply: *OK*.

Now to see Papà, because for the first time in years I'm going to be taking a holiday and things need to be put in place first.

I HOPE SELENE LIKES the water, I never asked but I wanted it to be a surprise. No daft emoji when I'd asked her to come in beachwear, she'd simply agreed – my kind of girl.

I've arrived at Meadfoot Beach twenty minutes early, so I can lift off the canoes and check everything's ready. I'm just pouring myself a coffee out of the flask when she arrives. It takes her a moment to realize it's me stood by the burnt orange Nissan Rogue.

I grin as she walks over. She looks delectable in shorts and a t-shirt. Her mass of red hair is tied back in a ponytail giving her the appearance of a teenager.

'Didn't recognize me without the Lamborghini?'

She laughs; it's the sound of tinkling bells. I love it! 'Not at first!'

'Yea, sorry about that, I should have let you know. This is a family car; we all use it when heading to the beach. I would have picked you up but I was working up until the last minute and I just thought it would be quicker this way. You don't mind do you? I've been coming to this beach nearly all my life; your car is safe here.'

'Its fine, I've got first-rate insurance.' She's relaxed and smiling and all of a sudden I'm as excited as hell. This woman's just got something about her that I really like.

'Can you canoe?' I ask.

'*Now* you ask?' She's laughing at me.

'I thought I would teach you if you didn't know. I checked the tides and wind before coming, so I knew it would be ultra-calm. If you haven't canoed I promise you, you're going to love it.'

'I went on a week's camp trip with school in my teenage years, and they showed us the basis of it. I don't intend to roll today though, because I didn't like that at all.'

'It's fine, the weather's calm so you'll stay upright, but if you do tip, just roll out and I'll sort the canoe out. You just do what you're comfortable and safe with. We'll also stay close to shore so you'll always be able to swim in.'

'Assuming I can swim.'

'Damn, you can swim can't you? I can't take you out otherwise, just too dangerous.'

She's grinning like a Cheshire cat. 'I *love* the water. I think in another life I must have been a mermaid, because I could stay in the sea for hours.'

I could kiss her right now. 'Do you mind helping me carry the canoes? I can drag them along the sand, but prefer to carry them.'

'Sure.'

'Also, we need to put these paddle jackets on. They're super lightweight, after a few minutes you'll forget you've got it on. Plus there's a secure pocket there, you can drop your keys into.'

'Cheers,' she says as I pass her one.

'Here let me check.' I lift her jacket up by the shoulders, it rises quite high. 'You need to make sure it is tight around the waist to stop it rising.' I talk hold of the buckle on the side and pull it tight. All the time I'm aware she's watching my face. Citrus aromas rise off her hair and skin, I want to draw in a deep sniff but refrain.

'Thanks.'

'You're welcome. Ready?'

She nods. As I'm at least eighteen inches taller than her, I take the back end of the canoe so I can make sure I bend enough to take most of the weight.

'You OK to jog?' I call to her.

'Sure!'

She quickens the pace, we need to do this trip twice and the sea is quite a way out.

'Will it be alright here?' she asks as we head back for the other one.

I turn to the side and smile down at her. 'Sure.'

We're finally on the water. She's a bit clumsy at first, knocking the paddle in at the wrong angle a few times and spinning circles until she gets into a rhythm.

'Yeah!' she cries as we finally start making way.

'Have you been to Torquay before?'

'No.'

'Do you know the whole coastline has been designated UNESCO Global Geopark status on account of its amazing geology?'

'Nope.'

'We're about to see some awesome rock formations. But the whole area is only one out of eight in the UK to be awarded this status. Everywhere around here has amazing landscapes, mountains and coastlines. It's one hell of a place.'

'You sound like a tour guide.'

'Oh sorry, Bella, I won't go on about it.'

'No, please do, it's great, like I've hired my very own tour guide. Carry on if you want me to leave you a rave review!'

And I do. We glide through the water and I talk and talk and talk, until I'm parched.

On the way back to the beach I don't want the day to end. I'm relaxed, happy and excited about my new catch. 'I know you said you wanted to meet in the afternoon, but could I please take you to dinner?'

She glances as me as she paddles. 'Can we wait until we're back at the cars before I answer?'

'Sure.' Drat, she's going to turn me down. Maybe it's too much for one day; maybe I should have waited to ask her out again in a couple of days. Normally I pace myself super-slow, it drives the chicks crazy, but I'm acutely aware I'm on a holiday deadline here and I've got to move quicker than normal.

Back at the cars, Selene helps me lift and tie the canoes onto the car roof rack. When it's clear we're done and it's time to go we naturally stand in front of each other. I want to burst out and tell her I want to see her again. I thought she'd had a nice time. But now I'm nervous, like I'm about to be rejected.

'Dinner can wait for another day, if you're tired.'

She gets lost in my eyes, going deep assessing my soul. Speak woman you're killing me.

'What do you want Giovanni?'

'What?' Damn, but that's a direct question. I never lie, but I often avoid the full truth.

'I mean, what do you want by asking me out? You know I'm only here on holiday, which suggests that you're looking for a holiday fling.'

Merda! How do I answer?

'Don't take too long to answer or I'll know you're lying.'

'Smart girl.'

'I'm trying to be.'

'OK, here we go. I think you're an incredibly sexy and beautiful woman. I would love it if you would spend some of your holiday time with me so we can get to know one another. Would I like a holiday fling, sure, I'm not going to lie. But I'm also a gentleman, so if you just want to meet up and go sightseeing, that's fine, we'll do that. But I would like to get to know you.'

Did I say the right thing? I can't tell. Her face is pretty closed down.

'Text me the address of where you want to eat, I'll meet you there at seven.'

Not what I was expecting, but a thrill goes through me, I love positive, confident women.

'I'll do that.'

'Thanks for a wonderful afternoon.'

I move forward to kiss her cheek but she steps back.

'See you later,' she says turning towards her car. 'Oh,' she turns back. 'Don't pick anywhere fancy will you? It's just I want to relax.'

'I'll bear that in mind.'

As I watch her drive away, I'm out of sorts. I'm excited I haven't ruined it, but I'm supposed to be the one chasing and yet somehow I think she just took control.

Chapter 9

Selene – If I'd met You First

THIS AFTERNOON WAS GREAT. My arms are totally aching now, but I don't mind because an afternoon on the sea like that was my dream pastime.

I've got my four evening type dresses on the bed, and I'm trying to choose between them. I want to look my best. You see I've decided I would like a holiday romance with Giovanni. He's not good at hiding the fact that he finds me sexy and wants to have sex. The fact that he is so obviously a Casanova puts me at ease, you see I don't want romance, I want fun.

I lift a pale-pink shimmery dress and hang it in front of me. It is lined and means I can wear it without a bra. I grin at my reflection in the mirror. Maybe I should go for something a little less obvious.

Throughout my education, and later my marriage, I moved as mother expected me to. I was studious, later I became career minded. Then I became a caring, conscientious wife, anticipating all of Mark's wants and needs before he even knew he wanted them. I have been a role-model everything... up to now.

Now I want to break out of my mold. I want to be daring and adventurous, and well a little bit naughty.

I lift up an olive-green dress, which makes my eyes pop with color. This is the one.

Giovanni is a player. I can spot them a mile off. Normally, I run a mile when I see one coming. But Gio being a player makes him safe, because I don't want any kind of commitment, not now, maybe not ever. I know for sure I never want to be squashed into someone's expectations ever again.

I wondered how honest he would be with me when I asked him what he wanted. If he'd told me he was looking for something long term I would have laughed at him, and then walked away. But in his cagey way he seemed quite honest. We'll see.

He's sent me the directions to a Chinese restaurant. He'd also asked if he could pick me up. I turned him down. Tonight, I'm coming home on my own. I'm embracing the daring side of me, but I'm not quite ready for anything else *just yet*.

Wow, but he's a stunner! I wish I could take his picture and send it to Shelley; she'd have a hot flush! He's in a suit, no tie, and his hands are in his pockets. He could be a model.

He crosses the restaurant to greet me and then guides me back to our table, which I notice is in the most remote part of the restaurant.

He pours me a glass of sparkling water, and I like that he's not trying to get me to have a drink so he can drive me home.

'You look amazing.'

He seems sincere. I smile. I did go to extra effort with the make-up, contouring – the works, a world apart from my appearance this afternoon. For the first time since we've met he seems a bit unsure of himself. I decide to rescue him.

'Tell me about growing up in Torquay.'

We spend three hours at the little table in the back of the restaurant, with its low light and discrete staff. The food's divine and the company, well let's just say hot!

I wonder what my life might have been like if I'd met him before Mark. What if we'd hit it off and hooked up? Would I be a different type of person? Would I have kids by now? Maybe if I had met him first, I wouldn't be so distrustful of men right now.

He didn't ask me what I want from him. Isn't that just like a man? Having told me where he thought this was going, he never once stopped to ask me if I wanted the same thing. Just as well all I want is a bit of fun, because boyfriend material he is not!

Chapter 10

Giovanni – Getting to Know You

AS I DRIVE HOME I realize I've spent nearly the entire night talking about myself. How had that happened? I went through the evening in my mind, promptly working out that Selene had adeptly switched every conversation into a question about me. She'd literally peppered me with questions all night long.

'And I didn't even notice! What must she think of me?'

Listening and being interested in someone is the best form of flattery. It's the tool I've used since my teenage years, to entice the ladies to remove their panties. Compliments and total devoted interest in them, works every time. The only time it failed on me, was when I'd hit on a married colleague. I'd seen a flicker of hesitation in her eyes though before she'd said no, so I didn't take it as a full-blown rejection.

How had Selene managed to turn the tables on me? Was she a bigger player than me? Nah, she couldn't be… could she?

Chapter 11

Selene – Where Poets Stir Your Soul

THERE IS SOMETHING ABOUT walking through woodlands that restores the soul. Calm transcends and encompasses me. I think if you pinned me to a washing line right now I could probably go to sleep. The exercise has raised my spirits, and positivity reverberates through every inch of me. I'm full of fancy, and at one with nature.

One or two lines of different poems are fluttering in and out of my mind, all jostling for dominance, but my grey matter is searching, like a secretary through files, there's one that's on the tip of mind that I'm longing to recall. As my feet carry me back towards Cockington Village, my eyes try to absorb every aspect of Manscombe Wood. The light flickering through the branches cast every shade of green, from deepest avocado to viridescent flows of grey, green and gold. My fingers brush against deep emerald ferns, and for a moment I wish I'd been born hundreds of years ago. Back then life may have been harsh, but has reflected through history somehow an essence of innocence. How I wish we could return there. Then I recall no washing machines, espresso, or Spotify, and laughingly admit that maybe I don't want to go back that much.

Bingo! Go memory! *A. E. Housman's 'Tell Me Not Here, It Needs Not Saying'* has surfaced. I rush through the words to my favorite verse about feet walking through meadows that will not remember them.

Manscombe trees will not recall little, insignificant me. Nor will the path remember my walking boots. But I'll not forget this moment, content to be set adrift from all I've known, to drift in the silence of memories and wishes. Wipe the slate clean and dream again – but this time of something new. Where shall I go, what shall I do?

For the first time since Mark sat me down and told me his truth and asked for a divorce, I feel at peace. Instead of being afraid for the future I am optimistic.

All too soon I'm at the cottage. I decide on a hot shower, chicken Caesar salad for lunch, and then I'm going to paint.

The day is warm so when I'm ready I set the easel up in the tiny court yard. I flick through my playlists and decide on popular classical, maybe a bit of *Swan Lake* or the *Nutcracker* will inspire me. Conscious that these holiday cottages are close together, I keep the volume on low. Too shy to paint in public, I've tried to put the woodlands to memory, but I've also taken hundreds of snapshots on my mobile, so I open it on one that I think is simple enough for me to tackle.

I'm not sure how long I've been standing in the mini garden, when I hear the patio doors glide open on the big house next to mine. Foreign chatter flows out. It sounds like two women. I catch the word 'bambina' and conclude it must be Italian.

'Hi there.'

I startle, and the paintbrush glides across my painting leaving a huge green smudge.

'Oh, I'm sorry I didn't mean to make you jump.'

There's a beautiful face surrounded by a mass of thick black hair, peering down at me from over the top of the wall, she's either a giant or stood on a chair.

'That's alright,' I say, standing in front of the easel.

'It's just my grandmother has asked if you would like to come around for a glass of lemonade.'

My face is clearly showing my surprise, because she rushes on.

'Oops, silly me. I should let you know that Nonna has rented the cottage to you, and she likes to meet the people she rents it out to. If you're busy we could do it another time.'

OK, that makes more sense. 'I can come now. As it happens I've wanted to thank the owner for letting me stay in this wonderful part of the world. I was going to contact the letting agency and ask them to forward my email, but saying thank you in person is much better. I'll just wash the brushes and then come around.'

'Perfect! The front door is open, just knock and come in when you're ready.'

I've been here three days, and the thought of a short conversation with someone other than the shop assistants is appealing. I'm not lonely, but it is nice to mix it up a little.

I knock, but although the door is ajar and I can hear people talking, I can't quite bring myself to walk straight in. Luckily, I'm spotted and the young woman rushes to greet me.

'Come, come,' she says. 'Nonna, Mrs. Hastings is here.'

I'm going to have to change my name by deed poll pretty quick, Hastings is not who I am anymore.

'Mrs. Hastings, this is my grandmother, Maria.'

'Please call me Selene. I'm very pleased to meet you.' I offer my hand to a fragile-looking woman, who is sitting on a chair with a rug over her knees despite it being a warm day.

She smiles, I notice a few missing teeth. She wags her finger at me and then beckons while leaning forward.

Very continental, I think, as we kiss each other's cheeks three times.

'Thank you for coming,' she says. Her voice is stronger than her countenance, and although her English is clear her accent is heavy. 'Sit, sit,' she urges.

I perch on the edge of the chair closest to her. 'I just want to say thank you so much for letting me stay in your cottage, I love it, it's so beautiful.'

'Prego.' Everything about her is soft and inviting, and I find myself instantly drawn to her. For lack of something imaginative, I ask, 'Have you lived here long?'

'Sì, long time, maybe too long.'

She doesn't elaborate and I don't want to pry.

'You have booked the whole summer?' It's a question, but she already knows I've booked it for twelve weeks so I guess she's asking me why.

'I wanted somewhere quiet to rest awhile. I've started an art course, and around here is so beautiful how could I not want to paint.' I smile, I hope it's enough of an explanation because it's all I intend divulging.

'The English Riviera, yes, it is bellissima.'

'Have you been here before?' asks the young lady, pouring what I think is homemade lemonade from a decanter into three glasses.

'No, it's my first visit, but I'm sure it won't be my last. I've fallen in love with the place.'

'Sofia can show you h'round Torquay if you'a like?'

'Oh, no, I couldn't impose, but that's very kind of you, thank you.'

I catch Sofia raising an eyebrow at her grandmother, and realize that she's relieved I have declined.

'Sofia h'is good girl, she would love to show'a you h'round.'

'No, thank you. I just,' how can I be tactful? 'I just want to explore at a leisurely pace and not have to worry about time or anything. I'm sure you understand?'

'We do,' smiled Sofia.

I ask a lot of questions about the surrounding area, and we happily talk for nearly an hour.

Maria speaks to her granddaughter in Italian, and Sofia stands up. 'Nonna is tired. She's going to have a lie down for a while.'

I jump up. 'Thank you for having me, it has been lovely meeting you both.' Straight away I see that Maria is waiting for cheek-kisses. I bend and kiss her with some affection. As I'm pulling up, she grabs my right hand.

Patting it gently, with her age-spotted delicate fingers, she says, 'You will'a comeback soon, won't you? Tell me h'owa your holiday is going?'

'I would love to.'

'Thank you for the lemonade,' I say to Sofia at the door.

'We can buy any lemonade we want from the shops or markets, but Nonna insists on only drinking the one we make ourselves. Hush...' she raises a finger to her lips, 'it's an ancient secret family recipe, don't you know.' Her eyes are sparkling and I get the distinct impression that the lemonade has been purchased from the shops.

I grin. 'Well it was lovely, thank you.'

Chapter 12

Giovanni – Jumping the Gun

WEDNESDAY SLIPPED BY before I had a chance to stop and think about my little firecracker. It has occurred to me that working from four in the morning till eight at night to tie up matters, in order to be able to take an unplanned holiday, might be considered nuts. Especially, as I don't even know if Selene is up for another date yet! I had my phone on the table all day so I could see if she sent a text, she hasn't.

Papà has been watching me out of the corner of his eye. He knows me well and knows that something is up, but he doesn't cross-examine me, which I appreciate. All the family have been on at me for years to ease up on the work load a bit, and to leave different aspects of the firm with capable managers, but that drive in me to tick all the boxes, to make sure everything is just so… well, it's hard to walk away from.

Papà nearly fell over when I told him I planned to take a week off work, he heartily approved and even suggested I take two – but that's a step a bit too far.

And now I'm wondering if I've made a mistake. Selene's not sent so much as a *'hi, how you getting on?'*

Unable to concentrate anymore I decide to go back to Willows.

I have dinner with Nonna, and then when she's watching the television I grab my laptop and continue working. When it starts to go dark, Selene still hasn't contacted me. I've got itching feet and can't stand still.

'Gio, stop pacing and come and sit.'

I turn from the window, smile and cross the room.

Maria pats the sofa next to her. 'Tell me what's going on.'

'Nonna, I think I might have gone a little pazzo.'

'Perché bambino?'

I look into nonna's eyes and wonder what on earth I'll do when it's her time to go. Nonna retired just after I was born so that she could take care of us, allowing momma to work full time. Basically, it was nonna who raised us, when momma helped papà run the business. She's been a huge influence in my life and her advice is always invaluable. What will she think if I tell her I've taken a week off to chase a bit of skirt? I cringe inwardly. Selene is more than that, and therein lies my problem.

'I've met someone.'

Nonna beams. 'Grazie a Dio, era ora!'

'Piano, piano, we've only been on one date... well, two, but they happened on the same day.'

'So... tell me already!' She flaps her hands at me.

I tell her how I spotted a beautiful redhead on the drive down on Sunday, and how she'd been in *Da Casa a Casa* on Sunday evening. How we'd gone canoeing and then gone out for a meal. I tell her the truth – that Selene has gotten under my skin.

Nonna scrunches her face up and peers at me. 'You've only met her four times and now you're planning a holiday with her?'

'I'll admit I haven't thought it through. I just thought if I was off work I could show her around. But she's not contacted me today, and I don't even know where she's staying so I can't send her flowers.'

'Tsk-tsk!'

'I know, losing my touch, right?'

'Flowers don't win a girl, Gio.'

'No, but they help.'

Nonna tsks again and fixes me with a scrunched up thought-filled face.

'What is it?'

'She's staying here.'

I jump up. 'She is?' I run both my hands through my hair. I never even thought about nonna's two cottages she rents out. 'Which one?'

'It's nine o'clock, you can't knock on her door now, it's not proper.'

'Nonna, please – which one?'

'Oaken View.'

I bend and kiss nonna three times on her cheeks and rush out.

'Pazienza,' she calls after me, but right now I don't have an ounce of patience in me.

I stride down the drive and turn left into what was once the old farm courtyard. Sure enough, Selene's red car is there. There's a light coming from the windows and faint music slips beneath the door. I strain to hear what she's playing, ah, Dreams by Fleetwood Mac, not a bad choice.

I go to knock on the door. My hand stops before I touch the wood. Suddenly, my heart is beating irregularly. What if she's busy? What if she's got company? That's ridiculous of course, there's no other car here. I decide to peek in through the window to double check.

Careful to stay out of view, I tip just my face around the edge. It takes a moment for everything to focus, and then I grin.

Selene is dancing. She's in a gypsy-style skirt and top, bright reds and oranges. Her skirt swishes around her as she twirls on her toes with her arms in the air. Her hair is loose and flowing around her shoulders. She's mesmerizing.

I notice a bottle of red wine on the table, and a glass half-full. I go back to her face, her eyes are closed. She's a vision of delight.

I don't want to intrude on her happy moment, so I walk away. When I get back to the house I send her a text: *Hi, I hope you've had a good day. xx*

She must have been waiting, because she replies straight away. I like that she isn't playing games.

Selene: *Yes thanks, nice day. How was yours?*

Me: *It would have been better if you had been in it.*

She doesn't answer straight away and I curse myself for my impatience.

Selene: *You could be in it tomorrow?*

Was that trumpets I just heard?!

I text back: *How do you fancy a BBQ on the beach for dinner?*

Immediate answer: *Sounds amazing.*

Me: *Great, I'll pick you up at seven.*

Selene: *But you don't know where I'm staying.*

I'm smiling as I text: *Actually, I've just found out you're staying at one of my grandmother's cottages.*

Selene: *Small world!*

Me: *So tomorrow at seven?*

I love her reply: *Yep, it's a date.*

One last text: *Night Bella xx*

Selene: *Night.*

Damn, still no kiss, but I'm getting closer.

Chapter 13

Selene – Temperature Rising

THE COURSE MODULES are two hours long. We're supposed to watch and absorb and then practice before the next one, but today I've played three already. It's just a bit too basic at the moment for me, I mean really – I know how to wash my brushes out! I can't moan though, it is titled step-by-step for complete novices. Which now I understand I'm not, as I did art in high-school and I do remember the fundamentals. I'm racing through the online tutorials, desperate to reach something more interesting, but also not wanting to skip any in case I miss something important.

I've been practicing while keeping half an eye on my laptop screen. I've gone through sheets of paper, all screwed up now and in the bin. Everything I've attempted has been lacking any semblance of talent. I wonder if it's because my mind is focused on a certain pair of come-to-bed eyes. I try painting them, but no amount of paint mixing can create the spectrum of color in his irises. I screw the last piece up and throw it at the bin. I'm done for today.

After I clear up – and wash my brushes with particular care, I grab a shower. There's only half an hour left before Gio comes to pick me up.

The power-shower is super, so relaxing as it pummels my shoulders. As I soap up and wash, I begin to imagine

Giovanni's hands washing me, touching my body, giving me thrills. A flood of sexual longing fills me. I put my hands against the tiles and stop washing to let the flood of water cleanse more than my skin. Get a grip woman! I grab the shampoo; I need to get out of here quick.

I decide on jeans and a t-shirt for the beach, and pick out a cardigan to wear when it cools.

To give my hair a natural wave, I wind it in a coil and pin it on the top of my head. When it's dry, I'll let it down and it will be bouncy and wavy. I put a bottle of red wine and two cans of the lager Gio had ordered at the restaurant, and pop them into a beach bag. I'm just rolling up a towel to put in there as well, when there's a knock at the door.

He's here? Seriously, how long did I stand in that shower?

I open the door to a smiling Italian Stallion. He's got Bermuda shorts and a loose fitting flower printed shirt on. He looks like a Californian surfer.

'Hi.' And what I mean is, hi, and wow you look good enough to eat – despite the terrible outfit!

'Hi.' He's devouring me with his stare. I feel naked and sexy and I bet I know what his 'hi' meant. I think of Joey from *Friends*, and his deep, 'hi, how *you* doing?' It makes me want to giggle.

'I'll just get my bag.'

'You're not going out like that, are you?'

'What?' I spin back to him, wondering what's wrong.

'Your hair.'

'My hair?' My hand goes up to touch the bun. 'What's wrong with my hair?'

'It's wet.'

'I know, but it'll dry in a couple of hours.'

'Meh! No-no-no. Non va bene.' He strides inside and closes the door.

I look at him in surprise, what's going on?

'You can't go out with wet hair.'

'I can?'

'No, no, it is very bad for you, you will catch cervicale. You must dry your hair. Mio Dio, if Nonna saw you with wet hair she would give you an hour's lecture on looking after your health.' He's waving both hands at me, with his thumbs clasped to the fingers – like he's making candle stick holders.

'Are we planning on seeing your grandmother?'

He's surprised. 'No.'

'Then we're good to go.'

'But your hair…'

'Will dry on its own without the damaging effect of hot air, *and* without ruining the environment by using an electrical item when I don't need to!'

'You're an environmentalist?'

Exaggerated sigh! 'Shall we go, before I change my mind?'

He's evidently perplexed, but nods and heads outside.

He opens the car door for me and waits for me to get in before closing it. I appreciate the gesture, not many men these days still practice chivalry – mores the pity. When it comes to the man being the head of the household I'm quite old-fashioned. I like, no, it's more than that, I respect, a man that wants to take care of his family. And having a door opened for me makes me feel feminine and cared for. Passé I know, but it's something I appreciate. Each to their own. Shelley is the opposite of me on that score. She insists on paying half the bill when she goes on dates, and bristles if they open a door for her. I have no idea how men are supposed to work out what females want anymore, we're all so different.

Giovanni throws my head a worried frown as he starts the car, and a giggle rolls in my chest trying to get out.

'Wet hair is frowned upon in Italy, then?' I ask, my lips twitching wanting to curve upwards.

'Very much,' he throws me a quick grin and waggles his eyebrows at me, before pulling out of the drive. 'Italians are very conscientious about their health. Wet hair and a cold draft are two things certain to raise a heated discussion.'

'Have you been to Italy?' It sounds like a daft question to my ears, but I don't want to assume just because he's very much Italian that he's been there.

'Many times, mostly for weddings and a few funerals.'

'Are your family based in one area or spread around Italy?'

'My grandparents were born in Foggia; most of their family is still based there.' He glances my way. My blank expression must say I don't know where that is.

'Foggia is in Southern Italy, pretty much opposite Naples – if you know where that is.'

'Yes, I can picture Naples on the map. What made them decide to come to England?'

Giovanni throws me an odd look, and I wonder what he's thinking.

'After the war, Foggia didn't have much to offer. The Germans and the British fought over it. The British got it eventually, but much damage was done. They set up a base there. Things changed. Agriculture almost came to a stop, there wasn't much food around. And then after the war, the British government was looking for people to come and work in the steel factories. The rest is history, as they say.'

'They did alright for themselves it seems, got out of the factories I mean, and into restaurants.'

'They got lucky.'

I sense there is more behind the story, but as he doesn't seem keen to share I don't pry.

'Would you like some music?'

'Sure.'

The Beach Boys' Good Vibrations comes on and I burst out laughing.

'What's so funny?'

'Nothing.'

'Hey, don't do that, tell me.'

'It's your shirt; I should have guessed the Beach Boys would be on your playlist.'

He laughs, it's easy and free, and I'm glad he doesn't take himself seriously.

'Shall I tell you something?'

I'm curious. 'What's that?'

'This is Francesco's shirt. He took one look at me as I was about to leave and frog-marched me to his room.'

'Why's that?'

'He said I couldn't go to the beach in black silk and that I was molto pazzo – which means very mad.'

I chuckle, 'Yeah, your t-shirt would have been better. What made you put on a silk shirt?'

He throws a look at me out of the corner of his eye. 'You did.'

Heat ignites my cheeks. I've never done compliments, and although this is a subtle one, it still embarrasses me. 'Well I'm glad he made you change, I shouldn't image silk and a beach BBQ go hand in hand.'

'True, but black brings out the best of my eyes.'

I look at him to see if he's being serious. His face is deadpan. I roar. I can't help it. The fact that he would pick a silk shirt, black no less, to bring out the best in his eyes just rubs my funny bone.

He joins in and we laugh, connected together in shared amusement.

Besides dog walkers, the beach is pretty empty. Giovanni is all prepared with everything he needs in two large bags, a cool bag and a wicker hamper.

'Can you bring the blankets?'

'Sure, but I'm not an invalid I can carry a bag too.'

He grins and passes me the smaller of two bags.

He must have a particular spot in mind because he heads off along the beach without any hesitation. 'It's not far,' he calls over his shoulder.

We head west along the shore, and after about fifteen minutes stop very close to the sand dunes.

'The tide never comes in this far, so the sand will be dry.'

I'm a bit in awe at how organized he is. He spreads not one, not two, but three blankets over the sand, all overlapping by quite a lot to give us a large area to spread out on. I've offered to help, but he's declined. I sit down, happy to take in the sight of his fine toned body as he sets up.

He ditches his beach sandals on the edge of the blanket and then digs a large hole in the sand in front of us. It's deep and wide. He walks around a little and comes back with some stones that he throws in the bottom. Opening the larger bag, he takes out a small BBQ. Before long the smell of burning charcoal fills the air.

Back on the blanket he grins at me. 'How you doing?'

Joey pops into my mind again, and I have to fight to keep the laughter in. 'Just fine, you sure I can't do anything?'

He shakes his head. 'Are you ready for a drink?'

'Yes, actually.' In fact I wish I had brought hard stuff instead of wine, because right now I fancy getting a little drunk. Sober me could never do what I wish I could do right now, and drunk me, well she's up for a bit of fun. 'I've brought a bottle of red with me, would you like a glass of that? Or I've got some larger.'

'Maybe later. I've got some Champagne, would you like some?'

'Oh yes please.' Champagne is the quickest working alcohol to get me drunk; it's the bubbles I guess.

Giovanni brings out a bottle and passes me two flutes. The cork pops and we both laugh. It's such a fun, party sound.

We clink glasses. Without warning, I'm lost in the depths of his eyes. My temperature rises.

'To a memorable holiday,' he says his voice a deep, warm rumble.

Oh I think it's definitely that already!

'If we're not listening to the Beach Boys, what do you fancy?' he asks playing with his phone.

'I'm not sure. If you were here on your own, what would you play?'

No hesitation. 'My classical list on shuffle.'

'Then let's listen to that.'

He grins and pulls out his phone. As he's searching through his music, I'm hit with the fact that I've done it again. Instead of saying I'd quite like a sixty's mix, or an

Enya album maybe, I've let him pick, to put him in his happy place.

I stare in my glass for a moment, churning over the fact that actually, Enya's melodic tunes would be perfect for this setting, and why didn't I say that? I make a mental note to stop and think before I speak from now on.

'You OK there?'

I lift my head and smile. 'Yep, everything is honky dory!'

Debussy comes out of his portable Bluetooth speaker; I begrudgingly admit that it is pretty cool to take in the setting with.

After Giovanni places what promises to be divine chicken and vegetable skewers over the heat, he sits crossed legged on the blanket and turns slightly to me, so his back is to the sea.

'Tell me something about you, Bella.'

'There's not much to tell, my life's been boring. Why don't you tell me why you live in London instead of the English Riviera?'

'You should stop that, you know.'

'What?'

'Deflecting the conversation to the other person, I'd like you to tell me something about you for a change.'

'What would you like to know?'

'Lots of things, but maybe… because of where I hope this is going, maybe you should tell me where your husband is?'

Flaming hot heat blazes my cheeks.

'Of course you don't have to tell me if you don't want.' He empties his glass and I can see he is struggling with something.

'You want to know if we hook up together, whether I've got an angry husband who is going to appear out of the blue and want revenge.'

'Something like that.' He refills our glasses.

'I'm just a bored housewife in your opinion, looking for a bit of light relief?'

'Bella, I honestly don't know what to think, that's why I asked. You're stunning, and if I was married to you, I'd never let you off on your own like this for an extended holiday.'

I didn't hear 'stunning' but I did hear, 'I'd never let you.' A shiver went down my back. I'm never going back into *that* situation where I'm not free to do whatever I like, never! His words are locked away in a box in my brain. The box has a label on it that says – reasons to stay away from Gio. As I lock the box with a key called determination, a little of my crazy need to have an adventure leaves me. Maybe dating Gio this holiday isn't such a clever idea.

My tone is flat. 'You don't have to worry; no duel at dawn will be required. Mark left me, and has set himself up with a new partner. You're in the clear.'

'Is the man mad?'

I can't help but smile, Giovanni is so shocked and indignant on my behalf.

'Maybe a little,' I say, 'after all he did marry me when he's gay.'

Gio turns the skewers over, before turning back to me. 'That makes sense, 'cos I don't think any straight man would let you leave.'

What he's said is complimentary, but all I can hear is the control. I knock back my drink.

'How did you end up marrying him, do you mind me asking?'

'My mother!'

He tilts his head to the side and throws me a puzzled look.

'Mark was the boy next door. My mother thought he was perfect, and basically she maneuvered everything.'

'And you went along with it?'

'I guess I thought she was right.'

'Do you always go along with everything?' His words are soft but carry a heavy question. My skin prickles. I get the impression he can see behind my mask. He's asking a question that he already knows the answer to.

'Not anymore,' I whisper.

'Good! Let's drink to that!' Before I can object he's filling my glass, but his I notice is still nearly full.

'Let's get this feast started shall we?' he says, opening the cool bag.

A plethora of culinary delights appears and is spread on a white table cloth he has thrown on the blanket. Salamis, pickles, bread and various cheeses – all my favorites!

As we eat, Gio continues to pump information out of me. Where I went to school. My first kiss. Which sports I like, and so on. The Champagne has long gone and I'm now drinking the wine, Gio has moved onto alcohol free beer. We're relaxed, sitting shoulder to shoulder, watching the waves on the sea and getting to know each other.

I don't think I've ever been more relaxed with a person in all my life. Not even Shelley, who can sometimes be demanding

I wonder if it's wrong, that right now I want to be naked and rolling on the blanket with a man who is practically a stranger.

Chapter 14

Giovanni – More than a Fling

EVERYTHING ABOUT HER tells me she wants me. Normally I would be smug and start working towards her complete surrender. I would be planning the where and when I got inside her panties. But I'm off kilter. I do want to get her naked in my arms, of course I do. Yet something is beginning to pull me back, telling me to go slowly, and to do things right.

But mio Dio, her eyes are dilated, her body language is exactly where I would normally want a woman to be. Yielding and willing. I could lean down now, and if the beach was empty (which luckily it isn't) and slip between her legs and taste the fullness of her. I settle for a kiss.

She moans into me. *My friend* flicks to life. Damn, but I want her, and evidently she wants me too. I run my fingers through her hair, wafts of vanilla float around. Her hands snake around my neck. She pushes her body into me; she couldn't be more obvious in her desire.

Her lips are soft, her breath whiffs of wine. Her fingernails are digging into my back. I roll us onto the blanket, I land on my right side and hook my left leg over hers, pinning her down. I pull back from the kiss to look at her.

Her eyelids are half closed. Her breath is quick, causing her chest to rise and fall. I smile at her and kiss the tip of her nose. She looks adorable, but I'm sure she's drunk.

'I hate to be a spoil-sport, but I think it's time I took you home.'

'Home is good.' Her words imply invitation.

I sit up. 'Come on you, let's get you back.'

I turn around as I don't want her to see my grin, oh but her pout is too cute.

She tries to help me pack up, but she's getting sand in the bags. I try not to bristle. 'Why don't you go for a quick paddle before we leave?'

She grins like a child. 'OK.' She takes three steps forward and stops and turns back around. 'Do you have Enya on your phone?'

'I do.'

'Do you think you could put her on for me, and can I borrow it?'

'Sure.' I flick through the list and press play. I switch it from Bluetooth speaker to phone.

'Thanks.'

As she rushes to the shoreline, I wonder if my phone will come back dry. It was hard handing it over. I wanted to ask where hers was but didn't want to sound irritable.

I turn the bags upside down to tip out the sand that Selene dropped in, and then carefully pack everything in the correct order. The pit where the BBQ was is filled in. I do a double-check, everything is clean, nothing left behind. I look for Selene. She's paddling. She seems happy. I leave her there deciding it will be quicker to put the stuff away and then come back for her.

By the time I reach the waves cresting against the shore Selene seems to have sobered up slightly. She gives me a shy smile as I approach. Enya's melodic tunes are flowing from the phone, which she passes back to me. I'm more than a little relieved to see it's still dry.

'Did you check my messages to see if I had a girlfriend?'

'No! Of course not!'

'I just thought maybe that's why you asked for my phone.'

'I didn't bring mine with me.'

'I see. Are you ready to go back?'

She nods, but I can tell she's on a downer.

I take her hand, and rather than head straight back for the car, we walk along the wet sand for a while.

'It's so beautiful here,' she sighs.

'When the sun shines.'

'I think even on a stormy day this place would take my breath away.'

'You take mine away.'

She peeks up at me, to check whether I'm sincere or not. I lean over and brush a strand of hair off her face.

'Are you always such a smooth talker?' she asks.

'Only when I'm with beautiful women.'

The answer is tongue-in-cheek, and she knows it, because it makes her laugh. Was ever there a woman who looked more attractive when she smiled?

'That's why I like you Gio.'

'Why's that?'

'Because you're a player looking for fun; and that's exactly what I need right now.'

I give her hand a little squeeze but I can't answer, because right now, playing is as far from my thoughts as Timbuktu.

Chapter 15

Selene – Play me Like a Fiddle

FRIDAY HAS ARRIVED so quickly, I can't quite believe it. Slight panic gives me a little shake, I've only come for twelve weeks and one has nearly finished already. The thought of time racing by without me getting my act together makes me feel sick.

Although, a Champagne and red wine mix probably has more to do with why I'm close to emptying my insides down the toilet. I'm also embarrassed. I've never thrown myself at a man in my life, and to have someone (who I know is a complete player) turn me down adds to the sickening slush inside me. I bury my head into the pillow and groan.

My mobile pings: *Buongiorno Bella, I have pastries and coffee. Let me in.*

Oh no, no, no. I'm normally a morning person, but not today. Right now my mouth is furry and horrible, and my hair – which I forgot to take out of the bun before I went to bed, is standing up in very odd shapes and angles.

I text back: *Sorry, not feeling up to company.*

Rat-a-tat-tat.

OH MY GOD! I can't believe he's actually outside the door.

I send another text: *Go away!*

'Bella, I'm not going anywhere. Come on, these pastries are still warm, you're going to love them.'

What to do? What to do? Shit, shit, shit. I run around the bedroom picking up my clothes where I threw them last night. I'm not sure why, because he's definitely not coming in here after rejecting me like he did last night.

'When the moon hits your eyes, like a big pizza pie… that's amore.'

Oh my God, he's singing! I bash my hair with the brush, trying to tame it. I decide nothing will do except for being wet again.

'When the world seems to shine like you've had too much wine…'

As I pull my head out from under the tap I hear him laughing. Swine!

'That's amore. Bells will ring ting-a-ling, ting-a-ling-a-ling…'

'Alright already!' I yell, yanking open the door.

'Buon giorno, mia Bella.' He walks in with such confidence I want to both hit him and snog him, and preferably at the same time.

I shut the door and march over to the table, where he's sat down and has begun emptying two paper bags. The aroma of strong coffee hits my nose first, quickly followed by pastries. My stomach growls. I slap my hands over it, treacherous body!

'Does singing like *Dean Martin* always gain you entrance?' I have to admit (strictly to myself) that his rendition of *Amore* was rather fabulous, and his deep voice cut through my resistance like a knife through butter!

'You should sit. These are so much better when they're still warm.'

I can't resist – two of my most favorite smells at the same time – it's just too much.

I rub my hands over my hair as I sit, hoping against hope that I don't look too awful.

'You look fine. Although, if you had taken my advice and dried your hair before we went out last night, you might look a little better.'

'Pah!' I don't know whether to laugh or scream.

He pushes pastries towards me. There's definitely no time to either laugh or scream. In a temper, I pick up an apricot Danish and chop down with anger-fueled relish.

'Umm.' My body melts as mouth-watering flavors of apricot and cinnamon wash over my tongue.

'Told you.'

I ignore him and reach for a coffee.

I'm too busy eating to talk. I make a point of not looking at him as I devour breakfast. Finished, I sit back with a sigh. I feel so much better. He's grinning at me.

'You good to go?'

'Go where?'

'It's a surprise.'

'Then I'm *not* good to go.'

'Come on, don't be a spoilsport.'

'You're seriously irritating.'

'And you're seriously sexy.' His mouth is slightly open, his tongue is pressed against an upper left tooth. I'd quite like to press my tongue next to it.

'Does singing and flattery always get you what you want?'

'Yes, of course, but only when accompanied by pastries and cappuccinos.' He sits back in the chair, confident, but with laughing eyes, so I know he's ribbing me.

'I could hit you right now!'

'I wouldn't do that, I might have to retaliate and put you over my lap,' he rolls his eyes, 'and goodness knows where that might end up.'

'You're impossible.'

'But that's what you want right? A bad boy, so you don't have to worry about hurting me when you leave?'

'Maybe…'

'Then stop playing hard to get. Go along with the flow, and have some fun.'

How can I argue? I throw a quick glance at my laptop, so much for a lesson every day, although with the amount of brain-fog I have right now I don't think I could have concentrated today anyway. Right then, my mind's made up. If I can't work I might as well play.

'What should I wear?'

'We're going to do some walking, so something comfortable and boots, and maybe a change of clothes for tonight.'

'Tonight? I never agreed to spend all day with you.'

'Stop being grumpy and go and get ready.'

I'm hovering between wanting to spend lots of time with this handsome hunk, and wanting to maintain control over my life. 'I'll get dressed for walking, but I want to be back here before six tonight.'

'Va bene, whatever you say, Bella.'

A sudden rush of excitement goes through me. All my life I've been put in boxes and I've complied. That didn't leave any space for spontaneity. Getting dressed, I take time to quickly text Shelley: *Being spontaneous, you're gonna luv the new me!*

A text comes back almost immediately: *Can't wait to meet her!! Have fun, and PS I'm coming down next Friday, whoop, whoop!* It was followed by a pile of firework images.

I text back: *Can't wait to see you! Gotta go, I'm on a mission to get Italian Stallion between my legs!!!!*

Another text: *Go girl!*

Chapter 16

Giovanni – Holding Hands

DRIVING THE SCENIC way across Dartmoor adds about forty minutes to the journey, making the drive an hour and a half. It's worth it. I can't believe there is anywhere more beautiful in the world than right here. And I want Selene to fall in love with it. I don't analyze why.

From the moment we hit the moors, Selene has been glued to her window soaking in the view. I put my chick-mix playlist on shuffle. The car is one moment filled with *Aretha Franklin*, the next *Take That*. It's not entirely my kind of music, well *Aretha* is, not so *Take That*, but I know women love it.

'Have we got long to go?'

'No, we're nearly there.'

'It's beautiful around here. I always thought moors were just flatlands covered in heather and rushes.'

'Like Wuthering Heights?'

'Yes, just like that.'

'I believe that's set on the Yorkshire Moors. We do have areas like that, but mostly it's a stunning mix of scenery. There is vast moorland where ponies roam, but there's also valleys, Bronze Age stone circles and medieval farmhouses. I love the rivers mostly.'

'Oh.'

'Have you read it?'

She turns her body to look at me. 'Wuthering Heights?'

I nod.

'No, I've seen the film though. Have you?'

'Yes.'

'You have?'

I can't help smiling. I don't know why women are always surprised that I love reading the classics. I started reading them to try and work out what most attracts women to men, then I kind of fell in love with them. I have a limited edition, or an original copy, of nearly everything considered a classic.

'If you visit me in London, I'll show you my book collection.'

'I don't make the time to read like I should. I miss it. It's on my list of things to re-introduce into my life, starting with this holiday. I've brought ten paperbacks along with me, and I've got tons on my Kindle.'

'What are you reading first?'

'Jamaica Inn, although I wish I hadn't. I read it when I was at school and thought it was so romantic and thrilling.'

'And now?'

'I find the writing style naïve and the heroine lacking. I'm disappointed and wish I'd not picked it up so I could keep the romantic image of it I had.'

'Life changes our perspective I guess.'

'It truly does!' That was a heartfelt answer. I want to know what caused it and I hope she'll tell me when she's ready.

I noticed she by-passed the invitation to my apartment.

'What else is on that list of yours?'

'Sex, lots of sex.'

I burst out laughing. That was not the answer I was expecting, but I like it a lot.

'I hope some of that sex will be with me.'

'We'll see.' She goes back to looking out of the window.

Soon after that, we're pulling into the car park for Lydford Gorge.

'At a steady pace this trail is about an hour long. Are you OK with that?'

She scowls at me. 'I'm more than capable of walking for an hour!'

'I know you would be normally, but I thought you might be a little wine-delicate today, that's the only reason I ask.'

'I'm alright, thanks.' The edge has disappeared from her tone, but my, she's a feisty one. I wonder if she's always been like this, or whether recent events have put her on edge.

I open the trunk and take out a small backpack, which I put on.

Selene raises an eyebrow at me. 'A backpack for an hour's stroll?'

'I'm afraid I'm a just-in-case sort of person. I have two bottles of water, some snacks, a first aid kit and two cagoules.'

'Is it going to rain?' She's looking across the sky, where not a single cloud is in sight.

'Aren't you English?'

'Yep.'

'Then you should know how changeable the weather is. If we have a downpour you won't be raising your eyebrows at me then.'

'True. But I think it's fair to conclude that we're not going to have rain today.'

'In which case the coats will remain unused in the bag, but at least we have them.'

'Can't argue with that.'

'Ready?'

Selene smiles at me, something thuds inside my ribs.

'As ready as I'll ever be.'

We head towards the path. We go through the gate and under the old railway bridge.

'Wow, I love woodlands.'

That's she pleased makes me happy. I take her hand in mine, and get a buzz when she keeps it there. We head off down the steep narrow pathway through the woody ravine.

There's a wooden handrail to the right, and steps have been cut in the earth to help with the steep incline. We take the path to the right when we come to a split. I want to show her Whitelady Waterfall. We stroll at a leisurely pace. Selene seems to be soaking everything in. Across the suspension bridge and here we are.

'What is it about waterfalls that take your breath away?' Selene asks.

'Besides the beauty and the power?'

'Yes. Is it the same reason why so many people love fish tanks do you think?'

'Shall I tell you something nerdy?'

'Sure.'

She's watching the fall. I place my arm around her shoulder. She doesn't stiffen or move away. I move my body closer so her back brushes my chest. I lean close to her ear and pitch my voice to low and breathy.

'There's a legitimate scientific reason why we love waterfalls. A waterfall releases negative ions, and when we're near them we soak those ions up as positive energy. Once they enter our bloodstream, our production of serotonin is increased, therefore making us naturally happier.'

She turns into my arms. Her head is tilted back so I can gaze into my stunning eyes. 'I think I would have liked you to be my science teacher.'

'If you were my pupil, I would have been sacked.' I didn't mean to kiss her on this hike, but I can't resist. My lips lower and find hers waiting for me. We're soft against each other, nervous and inquisitive at the same time. Her arms sneak along my shoulders and up to my neck.

I take the back of her neck with one hand, and the small of her back with my other hand. I draw her even closer. She moans and leans in. Unsurprisingly, *my friend* is awake and demanding action. I pull away. I have to. She moans as her eyes flick open.

'Are you playing hard to get?' Her voice is low, sultry.

'No, not at all, but it's driving a need in me that can't be met in these woods.'

'Let's go home then.'

I don't know what's wrong with me. Normally, I wouldn't hesitate, why do I want to go slow?

Selene puts a hand on my arm, her eyes are inquiring. How can I say no?

'OK.' My voice is a croak.

Just then another couple enter the gorge.

'Oh, hang on a mo.' Selene lets go of my hand and waves at the couple. 'Hi, I don't suppose you would mind taking our photo would you please?'

'Sure,' says the woman. 'Can we do a swap though, and you take ours as well?'

Photos taken and thanks given, I take hold of Selene's hand and start off again. All of a sudden I'm impatient to get home.

WE'RE NEARLY BACK at Willows, maybe ten minutes away, the journey has mostly been in silence. Selene has played with her phone most of the way and I know she's texting someone. I heard my phone ping not long after we started off and she told me she'd sent the photo to me. Besides that we haven't spoken much.

I'm beginning to wonder if she's changed her mind. It's not even two in the afternoon yet, is she really going to want to go to bed with me in the daytime and with no alcohol involved? I've had my fair share of women and although daytime sober sex did occur, it was never for the first time.

Out of the car I hesitate, she unlocks the door and walks in leaving the door open for me. I follow. Are we actually doing this? Is she playing a game, will she turn me away at the last moment? I close the door.

She goes into the fridge and brings out two beers. 'Want one?'

'Yep, thanks.'

She walks into the bedroom. My feet are rooted to the ground. I take a large swig of the beer.

She pops back out again. 'Are you coming?'

Not right this second, but I think I might be soon. 'Yep, sure.'

She closes the curtains.

I close the door.

We face each other.

There's no denying this is what we both want, yet despite being so attracted to each other we're hesitant. I put my beer down and kick off my shoes. Like my shadow she does the same. I drop my trousers, she her jeans. I bend and pick mine up, carefully folding them and placing them across the chair. Her face is like – what? I shrug, and start undoing my shirt buttons. She pulls her t-shirt off. With a finger and thumb she holds the top out, then, when she's sure I'm watching, she drops it on the floor. I place my shirt on the back of the seat.

Her lips are twitching in a smile.

I shrug. 'Can't help it.'

She steps towards me. Reaching up a hand she brushes my hair backwards, and then takes an even closer step towards me. The heat rising from her core draws me in.

Sod this! I scoop her up in my arms. She squeaks, but wraps her arms around my neck. I lay her on the bed.

I lean over her face. 'Are you sure?'

'Absolutely.'

I kiss the tip of her nose and then claim her mouth. Her moan is soft. When she's lost in the kiss, I use my left hand to pull off my boxers, and then I lie on my side beside her.

'Gio?'

'Umm?'

'Do you have… you know…?'

'I have protection, don't worry Bella.'

Selene closes her eyes and I claim her mouth again. Our tongues dance that dance of lovers, we explore. Our bodies heat up.

My hand is exploring, I'm not even sure if she notices when I pull her undies off. The pro that I am, I slip my hand behind her back and unclasp her bra. For just a second she startles. I pause, wondering if this is the moment she'll change her mind.

She pulls my head back down and kissing resumes.

My hand explores, very slowly, in between her legs. Her back arches and I use that moment to slip a finger inside her. She bolts upright.

'What is it? What's wrong?'

She's looking at me in shock.

'What is it Selene, are you OK?'

'I… I…'

'You want to stop?' I'm gutted, but I half expected it.

She shakes her head.

'Are you sure you want this?'

She nods and lies back down again, but as she does she turns on her side, so that her back is facing me.

I take it she wants me to kiss her back, so I do, I can be obliging like that!

Her cute little butt nudges into *my friend*. He flicks, he's been ready since I shut the door. Does she want something I don't do? Surely not? She's pushing her back into me, she's definitely telling me to go for it.

'Selene?'

'Uh-uh.'

'Turn around, Babe.'

With agonizing slowness she turns. I run my finger along her jaw bone, and then up her nose. 'When we get together I want to be able to see you.'

'Oh.' Heat radiates off her cheeks. Is she embarrassed?

I position myself over her and resume kissing. The tension that had built up in her begins to ebb. I take my time, waiting for her to fully relax. I know she's been married for twelve years but waves of innocence flow from her. When I'm sure she's ready, I slide in.

Her eyes ping open. I capture them with my stare. Stay with me, Babe. I move. Slow, sure, deep thrusts. Her eyes blink, but she keeps them open. I want to go crazy and pound the living daylights out of her, but I can see in her eyes she's not ready. I keep the rhythm slow and deep. I'm afraid she's still uncomfortable and not sure. I keep my attention fully on her face ready to withdraw if she asks me.

Gradually, her breathing gets heavier, she begins to raise and drop her hips in sync with my stride. Her moans are getting louder. Her eyes are closed. She's biting on her lip.

I can't take it. *My friend* releases, I grunt and collapse on top of Selene.

'Sorry, Bella.'

Her voice is husky. 'What for?'

'For not waiting for you, I tried, but I just couldn't hold it.'

Little pearls of laughter come from her.

I sigh, and roll onto my side, at the same time pulling her onto my chest. 'I just need a rest and we can go again. Next time I'll make sure it's all about you, Babe.'

She settles her head on my shoulder, although the day is warm, I pull a sheet over us.

She giggles.

'What's up?'

'Protecting me from drafts?'

'Ha, maybe.'

We're quiet, content to enjoy the moment. Her breathing is steady and slow, like she's about to drift off to sleep.

'Selene?'

'Uh, uh.'

'Do you prefer sex on your side?' I need to know, because if that is what does it for her, that's what we'll do.

She stiffens. I wait.

When it seems the cat has gotten her tongue, I prod, 'Tell me, Bella.'

She takes a big breath, and I realize what she's about to say is deadly serious to her. 'That is the only position I know… well did know.'

I have to take in what she just said, does that mean she's never had sex in any other position before? Before I can ask another question she adds more.

'I think it is safe to say that was the only way Mark could perform with me, that looking at my back allowed him to imagine a man, I guess.'

I want to say – that's the only position you've had – but I can't. I'm too shocked and I don't want to offend her. Another thought pops into my mind, 'Does that mean that the only man you've ever been with is your husband?'

'Yes.'

I tighten my grip around her. I'm filled with an urge to protect her. The injustice of a gay man marrying a woman is huge! I'm going to show her what being with a heterosexual man is like. Mio Dio, not only that but a full-blown horny Italian! She's not going to know what hit her! Mama Mia but this is going to be fun!

Chapter 17

Selene – Getting to Know Me

I CAN'T BELIEVE WE'VE HAD SEX three times this afternoon. Stallion is the perfect description for my Italian. I don't think I'm going to be able to walk tomorrow!

'That was John, one of my mates. He wanted to know if I was up to going around to theirs for dinner. I said no, that's OK with you isn't it? I kind of just want you to myself for a little while.'

'I'm not up to meeting anyone, so yes, that's fine with me. Although, you should go if you want.'

I'm in the kitchen making up a cold spread. He puts his phone down on the table and comes behind me. He wraps his arms around my waist and squeezes.

'Lady, I don't know how long I have you for, so every minute I'm able to be with you, I'm going to grab it.'

Warmth floods me. I feel wanted; it's a very heady sensation.

He helps me get everything on the table. It's fair to say we're both starving. Luckily, I have a week's supply of food in the cottage, so we have a hearty spread of different cheese, cold cuts, and salads. There's also grapes and pickles. Not to mention lots of red wine to wash it down with.

After the food, we curl up on the sofa with the wine.

Gio's arm is around me and I'm lying back against his chest. 'What do you want to do tomorrow, Bella?'

'Don't you have other things you need to do?'

'I was planning to go surfing, but I'd rather spend the time with you.'

'You should go surfing, Gio.'

He tenses under me. 'Don't you want to spend another day with me?'

I should hesitate. I should tell him no. I do neither. 'Yes, of course. But I don't want you to put your life on hold.'

'I want to get to know you, so unless you come with me I'm not going.'

'OK then, I'll go with you.'

He pushes me off him and sits up so we can look at each other. 'Tomorrow's plan is for an early-doors surf. I'll be leaving about five in the morning if I'm going.'

'I do mornings, that's fine. Where do you surf?'

'In lots of different places, but tomorrow we're meeting at Bantham Beach.'

'We're?'

'Yep, when I'm down here I normally meet up with John and some of the others to catch waves. Do you surf?'

I shake my head. 'Never fancied it.'

'But you love the water?'

I love that he knows that about me, after all our years of marriage I don't think Mark knows I love the sea.

'I'd like to bring along my paints and have a go at painting the waves. Going early will mean there will be clear light for me to try and capture the sparkle on the waves.'

'We should go slightly earlier then, and catch the sunrise, not always, but some days it can be stunning.'

'Oh yes, let's do that.'

Before I can say anything else, he has grabbed my face in his hands and is kissing me again. Linked together we shuffle into the bedroom. I get the giggles when we nearly fall over. He picks me up and fireman-like throws me over his shoulders like a sack of potatoes.

'Hey!' I playfully thump his back.

Plop! He drops me on the bed, and then he's climbing on top of me.

'Again?' I can't believe it. In the early days, Mark and I had sex about once a month, but when he finally told me he was gay, we hadn't had sex for eighteen months.

He doesn't answer. His eyes are full of tiny red veins as lust consumes him. Knowing he is this attracted to me sends my libido crazy. I want him, just as much as he wants me.

Giovanni's mouth begins to explore my body. My mind flutters between a thousand thoughts that come in rapid succession.

What would mum say if she knew I was having sex with a virtual stranger?

Wait till I tell Shelley, she's not going to believe it.

Does Mark touch Justin the way Gio's touching me?

Will Gio remember me after I'm gone?

'Argh! Ooh!' Time to stop thinking. 'Oooooh!'

Giovanni has been asleep for ages, but I can't drift off. In extremely slow and tiny movements, I maneuver myself out from his arms. I pick up my dressing gown and tiptoe into the living room.

Moonlight streams in through the window. I get a glass of water and then curl up on the sofa hugging a cushion.

I don't know how long I'm here, and maybe I was drifting off, because a sudden noise jolts me and I sit up. His feet patter on the wooden tiles, and then he's in the doorway, as naked as the day he came into the world.

He comes over and kneels in front of the sofa. 'What's up, Bella?'

How can I tell him when I can't quite pin it down myself?

'I think it's just too soon for me to be falling asleep next to someone.'

He searches my face, gives a slight nod and stands.

I glance at the floor so as not to be eye-level with a certain well-endowed part of his anatomy.

One minute later he's dressed and coming back towards me. He tilts my chin with his finger and grazes my lips with the gentlest of kisses.

'Don't forget to set your alarm.'

I'm so grateful he hasn't made a fuss. I smile.

As he opens the door he reminds me, 'Be ready at four, don't worry about refreshments, I'll have it covered. Just bring yourself and your paints. Oh, and a swimsuit so we can take a dip.'

'See you in five hours.' I do grin, how mad are we?

When I'm curled back under the duvet and snuggled into my pillows I can't help thinking about how crazy this all is. It is exactly the opposite of what I had planned for myself. Painting and reading, and getting to know myself. What am I doing… having a fling? Shelley's texts earlier told me to stop worrying, I didn't have fun in my youth, and it's about time I made up for it. But is this me? Is this what I want? I know I don't want love. I don't want commitment or to be tied down. Being with Giovanni is the perfect solution, isn't it?

But if that's right, why am I confused?

Why when I looked at his sleeping face, did I get a desire to want to wake up every day to that beautiful sight?

I switch the light back on.

I've brought a holiday diary with me. I'm supposed to be recording my spiritual growth in it. I flick through the pages. Random sentences fill the first few pages.

I never want to be tied down again.

I'm my own woman, I make my own decisions.

I'm in control of my life.

I want a new career.

Painting is a hobby.

I want to do something to help others.

The last page I've written on says…

I feel attractive for the first time in my life.

I pick up the pen.

I've just had an orgasm for the first time. I didn't tell Gio.

We had sex 4 times in 1 day! I didn't even know that was possible.

I want to do it again.

There's a wild side to me that's breaking out. I'm more alive now than I've ever been!

Chapter 18

Giovanni – I've got the Love Bug

SELENE'S STILL GOT SLEEP in her eyes. She offers me a little smile as I tuck a blanket around her knees, before shutting the car door.

'Go back to sleep, Bella. I'll wake you as we're approaching the beach.'

'How long have I got?'

'About an hour.'

She puts her seat belt on and then gets comfy and closes her eyes. Being electric the car is quiet, I leave the music off. I hear her heavy breathing within moments. I wonder if she managed to sleep after I left. I think I managed about three hours. I couldn't stop thinking about her. I've come to the conclusion the love-bug is worming its way into my heart.

I'm trying to hold back, to squash it, I've been hurt once and I don't ever want to go through that again. It's why I'm still single. It was years ago, I was just a boy really. Impressionable and innocent, that encounter left a scar on my heart, and a wound I never want opened again. Her name was Alison; we were eighteen when she finished with me. We'd lost our virginity together and for six months we had the best time. I thought everything was perfect, apparently she didn't. She tried being nice when she first broke up with me, but I got a little nuts and started stalking her, trying my best to win her back. I punched her new boyfriend in the face, broke his nose, after that she wasn't so nice. She blasted insults at me, destroying my confidence in every way. I changed after that. Got a little cold you could say. I paid escorts to teach me how to give pleasure, because I never wanted to be accused of the things Alison said ever again.

I throw a quick glance at my sleeping beauty. She's stunning, and I love her red hair, but there's something venerable about her character that's pulling me in. Selene was so nervous and timid the first couple of times we had sex yesterday, unsure how to move and hesitant about touching me. With the gracefulness of an opening flower, little by little her confidence had blossomed.

It's made me overly protective towards her. I also have this desire to make her happy. Damn, but she's gorgeous when she smiles, and I don't think she has a clue of how hot she is, which makes me like her even more. She's the very opposite of the bunnies that chase me in London, and the holiday girls that chase excitement in Torquay.

I wonder what the guys will think when I show up with her.

The hour's drive is over. I lean over and gently shake her shoulder. She sits up with a start.

'Sorry, we're here.'

'Umm, hum.'

I leave her to come around a little, and go the trunk. I take out a beach blanket that is lined to prevent it from getting damp, and a flask of coffee and two cups.

I open her door. 'Come on sleepy-head, it'll be worth it.'

'Better be,' she grumbles.

'Wrap the blanket around your shoulders to keep the early morning mist off.'

She leans back in the car and then wraps the blanket around her. I lock the door and then take her hand and lead her towards the cliff. We climb the steep path to the top. I know exactly where I want her to be when the sun starts climbing into the sky. We walk a little way until we reach an old tumbled down tree trunk. I put the lined blanket over it and we sit.

'Umm,' she sniffs the cup when I pass her the coffee. 'Smells so good.'

We sip our coffee and wait. Already, the sky is lightening.

As darkness is pushed away, birds begin to chirp.

Today is a good day.

The rising sun casts rosy hues over the horizon. It opens before us, and all at once it becomes hard to imagine the darkness that was there but a moment ago.

'It's beautiful,' she whispers.

I wrap my arm around her shoulder. We sit in amiable silence. I wonder if her heart is stirred to the same degree as mine.

The essence of Selene mingles with the bliss of nature.

'This is a perfect moment,' I say.

'It is.'

Seagulls take to the air with a flurry and loud caws and squawks, soaring and diving and claiming the air as their own. Hares race and hop across the warren. Selene arr's at the tiny leverets that stop and twitch their ears. A ship sails by in the distance, smooth and silent, full of mystery. She leans into my chest. I keep my grip around her shoulder firm.

Suddenly, I want to say a load of stupid stuff. Like – I love you, and let's get married. I want to laugh at myself because it's so ludicrous. I'm afraid to open my mouth in case crazy thoughts become actual words.

I'm saved from my temporary insanity when I hear cars arriving at the beach. 'The others are here.'

'OK.'

All of a sudden I'm nervous. Will she like my friends? Will they like her? We make our way back in single file.

'Hey,' I wave to John, who is unloading his board from the roof.

'Hey you, you're early aren't you?' Then he spots Selene behind me. His smile broadens. 'And who have we here?'

'Selene meet John. John this is Selene. She's holidaying in one of Nonna's cottages.' I don't know why I felt the need to add that, but it's done now. They shake hands.

'Nice to meet you,' they say at the same time and then grin at each other. Relief floods me. Of course they would like each other, they're both great people.

'Where's Danni?'

'She's going shopping with her mum today. She told me to be sure and tell you, that you'd better come around for a BBQ tonight. You're expected for seven, no excuses. Her words not mine.'

John turns to Selene. 'You're very welcome too, it's a casual event; you should come.'

Me and Selene lock eyes. She doesn't know what to do.

'Can we get back to you, Bud?'

'Sure thing. Just send Danni a text to say whether you're coming or not before two, then she can cater for the numbers.'

'Thanks.'

'You coming in the water today?' John asks Selene.

'No, not today. I'm going to set up on the cliff. I love the view from up there.'

'You're going to miss out. The onshore waves are crushing it today. It's going to be fun.'

'You enjoy, I'm going to attempt to paint the waves.'

'I've got a spare wettie in the back if you change your mind,' John adds.

Selene picks up her bags from the trunk. 'Enjoy yourself guys.'

We rubberneck as she walks away.

'She's the girl from the restaurant, right?'

'Yep.'

'You didn't hang about.'

'I don't have time to, she's only on holiday.'

'So… a holiday fling then. I thought you were off those?'

'It's more than that.'

'I can see that.'

'You can?'

'You keep looking at her like she's food you want to stuff, in fact, I don't think I've ever seen you look at a chick like that, not even Jojo and she was some hot ass.'

'There is something about her. I've taken a week off to get to know her.'

'What! Jeez! This is deep stuff then, wow that was quick.'

'I don't know if it's going to be serious, I think she's pretty determined it's only a holiday thing.'

'Right, but not you.'

I turn from watching Selene's disappearing back to look at my best mate. Besides Nonna, no one knows me better than John. 'No, not me.'

Just then three other cars with surfboards on the roofs pull into the car park.

'Saved by the bell, aye Gio?'

I grin at him, and we automatically high five. We hold hands for the briefest second as we hit. It's his way of telling me he's got my back.

Two hours later, we come out of the sea and head back to the car. Selene must spot us, because before long she's striding towards us.

'How was it?' Selene asks as we strip out of our wet gear.

'Totally stoked! The waves were awesome today,' answers Mike.

'Gio and I have been coming for dawnys ever since we could surf. There's something electrifying about the light and the waves,' chips in John. Selene smiles for a response, and then her eyes search mine.

'It was cool,' I say, and she seems pleased. I like that it was my response she was really waiting for. 'How have you got on?'

She's packed all her art stuff away already, and I'm worried she didn't enjoy herself. I shouldn't have been.

Her eyes light up. 'The morning was perfect for painting; in fact if I wasn't so tired I think I'd stay here all day.'

'Tired aye,' laughs Mike, nudging John in the arm.

'Tired is good,' winks John. I throw a towel at him.

'Are you ready for breakfast?' I ask Selene.

'Am I!'

I laugh, I love that she eats like a proper person. I've dated far too many bunnies who only nibble at their food. It's a pleasure to be with someone who openly admits they love food just as much as me.

'Hop in,' I say when we're all dressed and packed up.

'Where we going?' Selene asks as I start up.

'Just over to the next beach. Bigbury-on-Sea has this community that run a small restaurant. The foods great. It won't take long.'

At Bigbury we drive straight up to the higher car park, which is just underneath the café. There are tables inside, but only three, so we order food and then wait on the tables outside.

'What's that?' Selene points across the water.

'That's Burgh Island hotel. It was built by some filmmaker in the 1920s. It's a classic art nouveau building, made famous by the fact that Agatha Christie wrote a couple of books while staying there. You see that small building in front of the hotel?'

'Um, hum.'

'Well, that was built especially for her, so she could be separated from guests and write in peace.'

'Wow, lucky lady.'

Breakfast is lively and fun like it always is. I'm happy that everyone has simply accepted Selene, and that she seems to fit in. I study her face when she's talking to other people. It's like I'm cataloging her features and burning them to memory. I checked Nonna's bookings; Selene is here for the whole summer. I'm going to have to change my work style for a while, because as long as Selene is here I don't think I can bring myself to go back to the city.

Chapter 19

Selene – And Breathe

I TRY TO STAY AWAKE to no avail. I'm embarrassed when Giovanni wakes me up when we arrive back at the cottage.

'I'm sorry I wasn't better company.'

'No problem, it was a bit of a late night.'

We look at each other, I can see he's thinking the same as me – what now?

We get out of the car and Gio comes around to my side.

He breaks the silence. 'What do you want to do now?'

'Actually, Gio, I need a breather.'

'Sure. OK then… Look I'll be around if you want to get together, even if it's just for a coffee. I'm staying at Nonna's so just come around and knock.'

'I won't come around today, Gio.'

'Right then. I'll probably go around to Danni's tonight then, it's good to catch up with them when I'm home.'

'Give us a kiss,' I say with a wink.

He wraps his arms around me and kisses my forehead. Not what I really had in mind, but it's kind of cute.

'See you.' I walk to the cottage door.

'Text me if you want,' he calls after me.

'Probably not today, but I will if I change my mind.'

'OK.'

My back is burning. I know he's watching me go inside. He's not moved an inch.

I turn and try waving, but my hands are loaded with my stuff. He nods and gets back in the car.

After I shut the door, I lean back on it and drop all my bags at my feet with a proper clang.

I'm struggling. I'm caught between a rock and a hard place. It would be so easy to fall in love with Gio. Besides his dreamy looks and super fit body and boy those abs! Besides all that, there's something about him that's getting under my skin and stirring up a trillion sensations, longings and desires.

But this isn't what I planned, and I don't believe it's what I need right now.

I head for a shower. Once done, I wrap a towel around my hair and put my dressing gown on. What I need today is to read a gripping book and take my mind off me, and simply unwind and just chillax.

I make hot chocolate and curl up on the sofa with my iPad. I'm always buying books when they're on offer, so I literally have hundreds on here that I've not read yet. What am I in the mood for? I've finished Jamaica Inn, which I'd brought down with me in paperback. I'm in a mood for something more modern today.

I'm flicking through for ages, wondering why I can't find one that grabs my attention when I come across *Heart Bones* by *Colleen Hoover*. Oh, I've been meaning to read this for ages. Shelley read it and told me that she found it totally gripping. A little sad, but a brill read. This will do.

Within an hour, I know that this was the perfect thing for me to do today. Getting lost in Beyah and Samson's world was exactly what the doctor ordered.

Two hours later I'm still reading. I thought I might have fallen asleep, but the books too good. I pour some crisps into a bowl and pour myself a wine, well I'm on holiday after all.

Another two hours later, and my body is complaining. I go for a quick walk to loosen my muscles and burn off the calories from the crisps I've already eaten, and the chocolates I'm planning on having later. As I walk down the drive I notice Gio's car has gone, and I'm glad he's gone to be with his friends. This thing between us is getting too heavy too quick.

Back at the cottage, I decide hot chocolate seems better than more wine. I eat rubbish, biscuits, chocolates and peanuts. Waves of euphoria envelope me. I remember Gio's comment this morning about a perfect moment, and I know that today has been a perfect day for me. Lost in the pages of an engrossing story, I have been able to switch off and unwind, more importantly I've been able to stop concentrating on me. A perfect tonic for the soul.

After a while I decide to read in bed. Big mistake! I thought I might finish the book in one sitting, but my eyelids keep closing on me.

Shelley texts: *How was your day?*

I text back: *I'll call you tomorrow, just going to sleep.*

But texting has woken me up.

I toss and turn. I don't want to wake up fully; I want lots of lovely sleep. But as I lie there, Gio's handsome face keeps appearing and smiling at me. I imagine his hands on my body. My temperature rises.

Damn and blast.

I switch on the light and go back to reading.

Chapter 20

Giovanni – Not Her Dream Man

AFTER TAKING NONNA TO CHURCH, I send Selene a text asking her if I can pop around. Its fifteen minutes before she responds, but she answers with a yes.

'Come in,' she calls when I knock on the door.

She's leaning over the table, looking at paintings. 'Would you like coffee?' she asks without looking up.

'No thanks.'

I walk over and look down at the spread of paintings.

'Are these all yours?' I'm shocked. There are loads here. When has she had time to paint?

'Unfortunately, yes.'

'Why unfortunately?'

She straightens up and stares at me. 'I'm not very good.'

I take another glance over them. 'They look fine to me. I couldn't do anything like this. And you've only just started your course?'

'Well, I did do art at school.'

'You can tell, these are good.'

'Really? You like them?'

'Sure. I don't know if I like them enough to buy any of them, but I do like them, and I think you've got promise.'

'Thanks for being honest,' she laughs, and there are those tinkling bells again. Dio, what a sound!

'What's that?'

'What?'

'The circle in the middle of this painting.' I point at one that I can clearly tell is Bantham Beach, so she must have painted it this morning.

'It represents the man of my future.'

The landscape is the ocean and the beach, sand dunes filled with grasses, the waves with white horses. It's bold and vibrant and reflects Selene's energy. But dead center is something out of place, a circle, made from rings of different colors.

'How can a rainbow circle represent a man?' My heartbeat has raised a notch in speed. She's not included the surfers in her picture. But I was there, in that wave that she painted.

She leans over the picture and runs a nail softly over the colors. 'Blue is his soul, pure and true. Red is his passion, and green his ambition. Yellow is his generosity and orange his kindness.'

'And the purple?'

'Purple is for commitment, a lifelong pairing.'

'Does he have brown eyes, this man of your dreams?'

'I don't know what he looks like.'

'That's why you've done circles?'

'No. I might not know what his appearance is like, but I do know the type of person he is.'

I take my eyes off the picture and turn slightly to take in her face, trying to gauge her true meaning. She continues looking down at the painting, and just like that I'm drowning in jealousy, because this colorful man is patently not me. 'What kind of person is he?'

As she continues studying the painting, she tells me in almost a whisper. 'He's kind, sweet and funny. He cares about things, you know like the environment and things like that. But he doesn't just care, he puts his time and effort into helping others. He's honest and loyal. But the thing I love the most about him is that he acts like I'm the only woman in the world.' She draws a deep breath and straightens up.

My face must be portraying my current emotions because she gasps a quiet 'Oh' and puts her hands over her mouth.

After an agonizing pause she says, 'I'm only here on holiday Gio. This isn't love between us.' She waves a hand and points to me and her. 'I'm not looking for that right now. If you are, then well, maybe it's best if we call it a day, because I certainly don't want to hurt you.'

Could she slap me in the face any harder? My guts are crunching. I keep my face perfectly still. Years of training in the board room makes it easy to not show any emotion.

'I just want to have fun.' For the rest of my life, but I'll take right now... for now.

A relieved smile spreads across her face. 'Good. That's settled then. We are Mr. and Mrs. Fun Times from now on, because Mr. Perfect-for-me is someway off in the distance.'

'Fun it is.' I hate lying, but I need time to change her mind.

Bingo! Flashing sirens! On that last thought, comes the sudden knowledge that I want this woman. Not for a fling or a casual romance. I want the whole shebang: love, faithfulness, longevity.

'I've come over to ask you to come to lunch with me.'

'What do you have in mind?'

I'd quite like to take her home and introduce her to my folk, but I don't think she'll be up to it.

'Gio?'

'I was going to ask you to come back to mine, meet the family, have a traditional Italian family meal, you'd love it.'

'I don't think…'

I put my hand up. 'I know it's OK. We can go into town. There's a seafood restaurant I'd like to take you to.'

'OK, sounds lovely. When do you want to leave?'

'Whenever you're ready. I'll ring and book a table, and then when we get there we can go for a stroll along the waterfront and go in for food after that.'

'Awesome! I'll just freshen up. Take a seat, I won't be long.'

I don't sit. I stand and stare at the rainbow circles. I'd been surfing right where she's painted it. Does that mean her subconscious wants me to be her dream man? What can I do to make her change her mind and to see me as that person?

She comes out of the room in a light floral dress and sandals. Her hair is loose, and she's put a straw bonnet on. I notice there is no makeup, only a slight brush of red over her lips, nothing more. It's perfect, she's perfect. The thought of not being able to win her over makes my chest tighten.

'Ready,' she says. I love that it's only taken her five minutes to get ready; the women I date normally want two hours.

The drive into town is only fifteen minutes. I park in the owners designated parking spot.

'Are you allowed to park here?'

For a second I think about telling her the truth, then decide against it and go for a half-truth. 'I'm friends with the owner; he's fine with me using his parking lot.'

'Handy friend to have!'

I laugh. 'He is indeed. You ready for a stroll?'

'Yep.'

I reach out my hand and get a warm buzz when she accepts it. I've never been a demonstrative person. I think most of the people I know would have their eyes popping out of their head if they could see me now. But it feels right.

With palm trees, a busy harbor full of boats, a sandy beach, and a wonderful array of continental-style cafés, restaurants and cocktail bars, the waterfront is the perfect Devon seaside resort.

Selene soaks it all in, every now and then putting her hand up to check her hat is firmly on, as the sea breeze is a bit brisk.

'This is quintessentially an English bucket and spade resort, I love it. But with the palms and the yachts you could almost imagine you're in the Mediterranean.'

'You forgot to mention all the Michelin starred restaurants, but yeah, there's a reason it's called the English Riviera. I'm glad you like it.'

'I love it! Looking at all the boats out there today makes me wish I'd brought my paints along.'

'If you come back on Monday it will be quieter. There's a spot at the end of the promenade over there, where painters often sit. It must be a good angle to get lots of the beach in.'

'What a marvelous idea, I'll do that on Monday.'

'Do you want to become an artist for a living?'

Selene laughs. 'Goodness no! I'm never going to be talented enough to sell my paintings. But I love painting, so I'm doing this course for me.'

'I think having a hobby you love is important.'

'Yeah, me too. What do you like to do… besides surfing that is?'

'I play golf, but I wouldn't say I love it. It's not really about the game for me, it's about spending time with people I like.'

'Anything else?'

'Actually, you know what? I love dancing. I've not had much opportunity lately, but I love the waltz and the tango.'

'I thought you were going to say you love club dancing for a moment.'

'Oh, Bella, I love that too! You should see my moves.' I let go of her hand and wiggle my hips while pumping my arms.

Her laughing warms the cockles of my heart!

'Where did you learn to ballroom dance?'

I take her hand again as we continue walking. 'We were taught when we were about five by our parents. When I was twelve, they sent me and my brothers to have professional lessons. We all moaned like mad at first, but then secretly we all began to love them. Of course, it might have had something to do with the fact that one of the instructors was this super-hot Spanish lady, damn but you should have seen her move!'

'Why did your parents make you all learn to dance if you didn't want to?'

'At weddings and parties we always have a mix of classical amongst the other music. Everyone dances. Grandparents love to dance with their grandchildren. It's fair to say we all love it now.'

'That's such a lovely thing to do. We don't have that here in Britian do we, such a shame. I would love to have danced with my family. I mean we danced at weddings and things, but always to dance music, never classical. I think it would be lovely to waltz with your loved ones.'

I squeeze her hand. I want to tell her she can dance with my family, but I know that is just pushing too hard. Somehow, I'm going to get her to a family event and get my father to dance with her.

When we're ready, we head into the restaurant.

'Oh, how lovely. It looks very Italian in here, don't you think.'

'Yeah, a bit. I think the owners were going for continental.'

I wave to Paul, the headwaiter, and head over to our table. It's in the bay window with a perfect view of the harbor.

'I love the thread of blue and white tiles across the walls, and I agree, that is very Mediterranean, as are the gorgeous floor tiles and all the plants in terracotta pots.'

When we sit, she leans across the table and speaks in a hushed voice, 'It also smells divine. My stomach is doing flip-flops.'

I grin. 'Mine too. Do you like lobster?'

'I've only had in once before, but I did enjoy it.'

I turn and give Paul a thumbs up.

'What's that for?'

'When I booked the table, I told them we would probably skip starters and go straight for two lobsters. Paul's been waiting to check that we definitely wanted that.' She has a funny look on her face. 'Is that OK? I can cancel if you want something else, it's fine.'

'Lobster would be great thanks.'

'Good. Would you like Champagne or rosé with it?'

'Definitely *not* Champagne.'

I get up and go over to Paul and order the wine. I ask how things are going and get a three minute business update, before heading back to the table.

Paul brings over a bottle of Château Galoupet Cru Classé and an ice bucket.

'It's alright Paul, I'll pour, thanks.'

When Paul leaves, I smile at Selene, who is watching everything with sparkling eyes. She pushes her glass towards me. I pour a little in. 'Would you like to taste, Madam?'

She picks up her huge goblet style glass and swirls the wine before sniffing it. 'Umm, it's fruity.'

'Can you smell the peach?'

'Um, huh, and citrus and something else I can't quite put a name to.'

'Almonds.'

'Oh yes, almonds. You've had this before then?'

I buy all the wine for our restaurants, but I keep that to myself. 'Yes, I've had it a few times. The vineyard has gone organic now, which makes this rosé even more appealing.'

'So it's a healthy wine!'

'It is!'

'Well, I'll drink to that, fill me up!'

Waiting for the meal we talk about childhood holidays. I make her laugh loads by recounting different escapades with my brothers.

The lobster arrives smothered in garlic butter and lemon juice. The sounds Selene makes when she pops some in her mouth is adorable.

I'm busy talking while Selene demolishes her meal. I laugh when she puts her fork down and sits back with a sigh. 'Would you like some of mine?' I tease.

'Don't tempt me!'

We finish the meal with lemon ricotta cake and espressos.

'Oh my goodness, that was my food heaven,' she says when we're finished.

'I'm glad you enjoyed it.'

'Will you let your friend know that I think the restaurant is wonderful and the food to die for?'

I grin. 'I will. Are you ready to go?'

'Um, hum,' she nods.

I wave at Paul and shout thanks, on the way out.

Outside, Selene grabs my hand looking earnest. 'Don't you pay?'

I bend down to whisper in her ear like I've got a secret. 'I have a tab.'

'Oh, that makes sense I guess, if you come here all the time. So what, do you like get an invoice at the end of the month?'

'I do.'

'That makes life easy. Although, I'd never do it because I'd be eating out all the time, and have no idea how much of a bill I'm racking up. Thank you by the way, for paying. I appreciate it; it's very kind of you.'

'It's not kind at all. I have every intention of extracting payment out of you this evening.'

'Really? Well I had better pay a visit to the ATM then.'

'That's not the kind of payment I was hoping for.'

'Oh yeah, and exactly what payment would you like?'

I whisper in her ear how I want to kiss every inch of her body, and then some more intimate things. She blushes but she's smiling.

'We'd better get home then because that sounds like it might take some time.'

Chapter 21

Selene – Lust Paradise

I'M IN LUST PARADISE. Last night was so much fun. Giovanni and I did all sorts of things I've never done before, like having sex on the kitchen table – Gio said it's only fair to christen all the furniture in the cottage, and that's what we attempted to do. It was lusty and it was fun. One minute we were playing around like kids, the next it was lust central.

Like Cinderella, at midnight he got up and went home. I hadn't asked him to, but I appreciated that he did. Sleeping together just seems too much like what a proper couple would do. And this is a holiday fling and not a proper romance.

I've asked for a little space today. I need to do a few more of my courses. He said he would do some light work, emails and things so I don't think he was too let down.

I'm cooking for him tonight. I'm going to steam salmon in a bag in the oven, boil Jersey potatoes and serve it with asparagus and homemade parsley sauce. I'm looking forward to being the one supplying the food for a change. I've learned that he's very much a foodie, and that he's very particular. He's going to be a challenge to cook for when he's used to fine dining, but I like a good challenge.

I've been giving Shelley updates on the phone and she's had lots to say about everything. It will be great to talk face-to-face again when she arrives on Friday. For now I need to do my lessons and get some practice in. I've decided I'm going to try and paint Giovanni from the photo taken at the waterfall. I love the photo. He has his arm around me and we're both smiling. We look relaxed, you'd think we'd been a couple for years.

Six o' clock arrives too quickly. I don't know where the day went. The food is prepared, but I won't cook it until we're almost ready to eat.

Giovanni sent a text earlier to say he's running a little late, and that's perfect for me. I shower for a long time. I want to be fresh as a daisy for his very explorative tongue!

'Ciao, Bella.'

Perfect timing. 'Hi handsome, you had a good day?'

We look at each other and at the same time, and burst out laughing the greeting sounding stereotyped, and ordinary, like a married couple.

When we're cooling down, he grabs my face and brings his lips to mine. The kiss is deep and intimate, searching and sexy with absolutely nothing 'married' about it. I melt into his body. Every part of me has begun to tingle. I push him away before I get too heady.

'Dinner first.' I wag my finger at him.

Dinner is a success, and I'm relieved to see him wolf it down.

'Would you like to watch a film?' I ask after we've washed up.

'Sure, what do you have in mind?'

'If you're OK with it, I've spotted a film on Netflix called Wild Mountain Thyme. It's definitely chick-flick, but it's got Christopher Walken and Emily Blunt in it, so I think it'll be good.'

'What's it about?'

'Not too sure, but it's set on a farm in Ireland.'

'Christopher Walken has an Irish accent?'

I giggle. 'He does.'

'Well then, we've got to see it.'

I wasn't sure how much of the movie we would watch. I half expected Gio to start getting amorous about twenty minutes in. But the film was sweet and held our attention. Besides moving to refill our glasses, we stayed glued together on the sofa. Gio is lying with his back to the sofa cushions, and me lying with my back against him. His arm is draped over my waist the entire time.

It's a deliciously comforting position. In all the years I was married Mark never held me like this. I'm beginning to realize just how much I have missed out on.

There's a part in the film when someone says, 'Bye-bye my Daddy.' I catch a hard lump in my throat and twist around to look at Gio. He glances down at me. Both our eyes are brimming with tears.

We share an uneasy laugh and turn back to the film. Gio wraps his arm tighter around me.

At the end of the film I'm crying. Gio reaches for a box of tissues that luckily is on the coffee table. We sit up. He keeps an arm around my shoulder and waits for the waterworks to stop. I'm embarrassed.

He leans his head against mine. 'It was a happy ending, what made you cry?'

I swallow the lump in my throat so I can talk. 'Because she knew exactly what she wanted and she went after it until she got it.'

'I guess a lot of people would have given up.'

'My dad told me when I was little that anything worth having is worth fighting for.'

'I'd agree with him.'

'But that's only good if you honestly know what you want.'

'You have a point.'

We discuss the film and the different aspects that we liked.

After a space of silence, Gio stands up and offers me his hand, which I take.

He leads me into the bedroom.

Giovanni undresses me. Slowly, with care and a tender touch. Every time his fingers caress my skin, tingles race over my body.

When we're naked we stand in front of each other for a moment not touching. We're using our eyes to pull us together. *Debussy* floats in quietly from the other room. Besides the stirring music there is nothing except Gio and me. I have no thoughts of tomorrow or yesterday.

My mind is empty except for the need to be made one with this wonderful man.

His full attention is in his stare. I am 'seen' and validated. Something in my soul shifts and changes and I'm aware that fun has just switched gears and become serious.

I catch my breath.

'What?' he asks.

I can't answer. I don't want this. I want to be independent and free. I don't want to become the other half of someone... not yet, not so soon. Yet, my heart is thumping. I want to disappear into his arms. I want two to become one.

'Selene, what's wrong?' Concern floods his features, his hand reaches for me.

'Kiss me, Giovanni, kiss me.'

For the briefest moment, confusion flickers in his eyes, but then he's pulling my head towards him, and I'm lost in the softness of his full lips.

We stand; Leonardo's statues of unashamed nakedness. I have never been comfortable naked, but in this moment I don't seem to notice. His lips move away from mine, and I instantly want them to return. I want to taste him, but his head has moved lower. He's kissing my neck. Shivers make my nipples ping to attention. He moves down again, kissing the nape of my neck, my shoulder, my breast.

I moan. He nudges us towards the bed. I lie down. All the time he is kissing, sucking and nibbling my breasts. His hands are roaming. I groan and arch my back.

'Umm, you like that?'

'Ugh huh.'

'Do you like this?' His hand slides up my thigh. I'm tingling like popcorn getting ready to burst.

He chuckles to himself.

His kisses travel south. Over my stomach. Onto my thigh, down to my knee. And then… back up again on the inside of my thigh. He pushes my legs apart.

My hands form fists, scrunching the covers, like that will stop me from shooting off the bed.

When his tongue finds my most private place I squeal. I think Gio loves that I've never done anything like this before, and he's taking delight in trying different things to find out what I like.

I've got to be honest, I pretty much like it all!

'OH MY GOD!' I'm sorry God, I can't help calling your name, but this is sooo.. 'Argh.' You'd think someone was killing me. I sincerely hope Maria can't hear me next door. Gio has slipped a finger in beside his tongue. He's rubbing a spot that's causing my womb muscles to start contracting. Oh here we gooooo!

Gio takes a drink and grins at me. I'm panting, still clutching the covers. How on earth did I not know sex could be this good?

Giovanni climbs over me. Our eyes stay locked at he pushes into me, his hands are on either side of the pillow next to my head. Pools of longing and lust connect us. I believe I'm the only thing in his world that matters. I'm his center, his universe – and he's mine.

I arch, but I keep eye contact. This is Gio's thing, watching my expression, ensuring I am enjoying myself, it's so heady, and sometimes it's almost too much.

I start to move with him. Arching my back as he pushes in, lowering it as he pulls out. Back and forth we sway. Back and forth. Back and forth.

Gio explodes with shivers and groans and flops over me. He mutters sentences to me in Italian which I don't understand. It doesn't matter that I don't know what he's saying. I know what he means, because Gio is home to me, and I think I am home to him.

Much later, when he goes to kiss me and get out of bed, I grab his hand.

'Stay.'

He doesn't say anything, just sinks back into the pillow and pulls me into the crook of his arm so my head is resting on his chest.

'Buona note, Bella.'

'Night, night, Gio.'

Just as I'm drifting off to sleep, he whispers in my hair. 'I will fight for you forever.'

Chapter 22

Giovanni – What's Going On?

COMPREHENSION – THE ABILITY TO UNDERSTAND... something. Merriam-Webster dictionary describes it as the act (or action) of grasping with the intellect, in another word, understanding. I have an IQ of 132 and could have joined Mensa if I had been inclined. I didn't, I always had too much to do.

Selene is sleeping, and I'm lying here studying her face. Just a moment ago I was walloped with the knowledge that I'm in love. I almost laughed, dismissing the revelation that has been brimming under the surface for the last couple of days. Love and my lifestyle don't go together. I'm not looking for love, or anything that entails, definitely not looking for commitment or relationship. Not me! Not the old me anyway.

Eureka moment!

Today I am a brand new man.

Yesterday, the possibility of falling in love in less than a week would have sounded ludicrous.

News flash!

Today, I'm a true believer.

Why? Because something just happened between us, that's hard to put into words. I've been having sex since my youth, and I've had it *a lot*. But I've never experienced anything like this, or been so connected to a person in my life. For the first time I wish I was a poet so I could find words to catch the intimacy and naked attraction we tasted. Separately, we exploded into a trillion pieces, as one we were rebuilt and remolded. The furnace of our lives now flows from the same flame.

Souls entwined. A new creation.

Her breath flows in ethereal wisps and brushes my face, and I realize that I want to feel her breath every time I wake up. There's no debate, I don't offer myself a choice. I'm in love with a stunning red-headed painter. This tiny firecracker has stolen my heart. A cog has ticked over in my brain, truly aligning with my heart for the first time in my life.

What am I going to do? I need to bring her to a point where she surrenders to the passion between us, but how can I when she has such a high wall around her?

I ease myself out of bed as carefully as possible trying not to wake her. I leave her a note on the table letting her know I'll be back later with breakfast.

I need a run. I always have my clearest thoughts when I'm running. In London I run in my gym, but that has no comparison to being in Cockington and being able to run in the country.

I unlock the door at Willows and let myself in. I'm upstairs and dressed in no time. As I'm heading for the kitchen door to go, Nonna's voice comes floating through from the front room.

'Gio, vieni qui.'

I go in and kiss her three times on each cheek. 'Buongiorno Nonna, what are you doing up at six thirty in the morning?'

'My bones h'ache a lot'a these days if I stay h'in one position for too long. Where 'ave you been?'

I sit down on the chair next to hers. I have a good idea she knows exactly where I've been. 'I've been with Selene.'

'Pensavo che i tuoi brevi romanzi fossero finite?'

'This isn't a short romance for me, Nonna. I like her.'

She's frowning and twisting her fingers together, showing how unhappy she is.

'I'm sorry that she is one of your summer tenants, but Nonna,' I lean forward and take hold of her hands. 'I *really* like her.'

'You 'ave only known her a week.'

'I think it was love at first sight for me, it just took me a few days to understand what it was.'

Nonna throws my hands away and rants at me in Italian. Her hand waving and gesturing is emphatic, her voice very loud. I'm worried that Selene will hear it.

'Shush, Nonna.'

'Don't'a you shush'a me, bambino!'

'It's a bit early to get all dramatic.'

She goes off on another rant, waving her fist at me and occasionally biting her knuckle for good measure.

'Haven't you met her? She's lovely.'

She sighs and sits back in her chair, but her lips are still pursed tight.

'Why don't you approve of her?'

'Lei è sposata!'

'He's asked her for a divorce, Nonna. She's free to start a new relationship.'

The wind eases out of her sails, and her shoulders drop about three inches from where they'd almost been hugging her jawline.

'She's special, if I can win her heart I might even get married!'

Nonna raises one eyebrow, skepticism in every fold of her many lines. 'Quel giorno mangerò il mio cappello!'

I bark a laugh. 'Then I'd best get you a hat made out of biscotti!'

She playfully slaps my arm.

'Can I get you anything before I go for my run, Nonna?'

'No grazie. Teresa will'a be here at seven.'

I kiss her on the forehead and head off.

Thoughts of her eating her hat on my wedding day fill me with amusement as I jog down the country lanes, as does the image of my friends and families faces when tell them I'm getting married.

I want to get married!

I skid to a sudden halt. What's going on with me? Am I mad? I've only known her a week and already I'm thinking of marriage; no wonder Nonna had a go at me.

I start off again, determined to slow my new impetuous-self down.

Two hours later, I'm showered and changed and turning up with a selection of different pastries and two cappuccinos.

Selene is up and also showered and dressed. I love that she's a morning person. Most of my previous relationships, with Jojo being the exception, have been with women who don't think the day starts until noon.

'Buongiorno, Bella.' I kiss her forehead and put the bag and coffee tray on the table. 'How you feeling today?' I'm worried her sad mood from last night might still be with her.

'Fine, thanks. You?'

I grin and wink. 'I'm very good.'

We eat, drink and talk. It's comfortable like we've known each other for years.

'What would you like to do with the rest of the week?'

She averts her eyes and concentrates on the table, not a good sign. 'You want more time on your own?'

She lifts her face and smiles at me. 'Yes. Please don't be offended, I'm having a great time, and I love spending time with you. But I came here with a mission, and I feel like I'm letting it slip through my fingers.'

'OK. Do you want to see me again?' My heart thudding so hard.

'Yes, oh God – yes! I just want to slow it down a bit, is that alright?'

'Sure Bella. This is your holiday; you should do exactly what you want with it.'

'Thanks for understanding.'

I don't understand. How can she not feel the same way that I do? I never want to be away from her. Merda! This is hard.

'Do you have an idea when you'd like to see me again?'

'Not until next week.'

Merda! How can I go that long? And I've taken the week off, what an idiot I am. I'll have to start switching things around again. 'Can't we do something together at the weekend?'

She shakes her head. 'My friend Shelley is arriving on Thursday night and she doesn't leave until after lunch on Sunday, so it will have to be next week.'

'How about we do something altogether?'

'I'm not sure. She's only here a couple of days and I want to give her my full attention, I don't want her to feel like a spare wheel.'

'Then we'll join up with my friends too, so we're in a group.'

'Why don't you text me your idea on Friday, and I'll ask her what she wants to do?'

'Sounds like a plan. Right then, I won't keep you.'

We stand and she walks towards the door with me. It feels a bit awkward.

She stands on her tiptoes and comes in for a kiss. There's nothing uneasy about the kiss. As soon as our lips touch, she melts against me. My arms tighten around her. Merda, but I don't want to let her go.

After a long smooch, she pulls back.

'Ciao Bella, call me if you need anything.'

'I won't need anything, but thank you.'

She stands in the doorway, watching me until I'm around the wall and out of sight. I'm finding it hard to breathe.

Chapter 23

Selene – Don't Hold Back Granma

I'VE GOT THREE DAYS to myself before Shelley arrives. I plan to get through at least nine more art sessions and get tons of practice in. Before I start I pull out an A4 notepad. I'm planning on writing lots of lists. Things I want to do in my life, things I want to avoid. Places I want to visit and a list of things I enjoy.

I'm hoping after all the lists are written I might get a clear picture of the things that make me tick. Whatever that is, that's the career I'm going to go after, and the life I'm going to pursue. I need to decide what it is I want because until I do I'm going absolutely nowhere.

If I could wave a wand and be living my dream life, what would it look like? 'Umm.' Tough one. I think I would like my own home without a mortgage, this represents security to me, there's nothing safer than bricks and mortar. Do I want a husband? Kids?

'Umm.' I chew the tip of my pen. I do. I can't imagine living my whole life on my own, although I know some people do and they're happy. I think I would like three children, and that means having a husband too. The man I was dreaming of while I was painting is an easy list of requirements.

'Where do I want to work?' This is harder. The only thing giving me any kind of passion at the moment is the thought of doing charity work. Is it possible to get a job and work full-time for a charity? I start online searches. Wow, there are loads of charities looking for employees. I must be stupid! Of course they run just like businesses and need employees. I start writing down a list of positions that are currently open with *Oxfam*. I'm getting more and more excited by the minute. This is definitely for me.

I thought the list process would take me an hour – it takes four, by the end of it though I'm feeling positive. The shape and form of the future me is beginning to crystallize, it's exciting!

SOMETHING PRODS ME to go and visit Maria the next day. I tap quietly on the door in case she's having a nap. A lady I've not met before opens the door.

'Hi, I just wondered if Maria was up for a visit.' The woman's unresponsive face prompts me to add, 'I'm Selene, renting the cottage next door.'

'Wait here please. I'll just check she's up for receiving visitors.' She's gone only moments. 'Please come in.'

I follow the woman into the living room, where Maria is sitting on a high-backed chair, and despite the warmth of the day, has a blanket over her knees.

'Can I get you a drink?'

I assume this lady is some sort of caretaker. 'A glass of water would be lovely, thank you.'

Kisses exchanged, I sit on the sofa near Maria.

'How h'is your holiday going?'

'Wonderful. I love it around here. There are so many sites of beauty I'm a bit overwhelmed.'

We idle chit-chat for half an hour, then Maria fixes me with an inquisitive stare and I wonder what's coming.

'Why h'is your husband not with you?'

I rub my wedding band, which for some odd reason I still haven't removed. For a moment I think about lying and telling her he's working hard and couldn't come on holiday. Instead, the truth flows out. In under ten minutes, I've summed up my empty life and painted a fairly accurate picture of both Mark and my mum.

I instantly feel guilty for burdening this sweet old lady with my woes. She reaches out a hand, which I take. She squeezes it and tears sting my eyes.

'Life h'is rarely what'a we think it will be,' she says, letting go of my hand and reclining in her chair once more.

'I guess that's what I'm learning.'

'My grandson likes you, rather a lot'a.'

I blush. 'I like him too.'

'But you h'are not divorced yet, so you are *not'a* free.'

I can't help but bristle, her tone was quite accusatory.

Before I can respond, she continues. 'When you h'are divorced, I think'a you will'a be good for Giovanni, he finds h'it hard to settle you know. I think it h'is because he doesn't know what he's'a looking for.'

Panic hits my chest. I haven't even signed my decree nisi yet, I have no intention of settling down into a serious relationship. I don't know what to say to her.

'It h'is as I thought,' Maria says with a sigh. 'You do not love him, and you 'ave no intention of staying h'around. That h'is a pity. I thought per un piccolo momento, Dio had answered my prayers,' she kisses her rosary, 'to bring 'appiness and stability to my Giovanni.'

'I'm sorry.' What else can I say?

'Don't do that!'

Her tone is sharp and I'm rattled. 'What?'

'Don't make h'excuses or h'apologies for the life you choose. You h'are not ready for a new relationship that h'is understandable, you do not 'ave to apologize to anyone. *Anyone*, do you hear?' She's very loud and emphatic and wagging her finger at me.

I think my face is on fire. But mingled with embarrassment is an appreciation for what she's saying. She's basically telling me to accept who I am and isn't that why I'm here, to find that out?

'Tell'a me more about your mother.'

My face reflects my surprise, and a pile of questions jump into my mind, mainly – what for?

'Humor me, Selene, take a chance h'and speak honestly with h'an old woman you don't know and who you will probably not'a meet again except to say arrivederci.'

I don't know why she wants to know, but my mouth opens and I start pouring out my upbringing. How I was always a daddy's girl, how mum resented it and took no bones about telling me. How when dad died in a car accident, we had been thrown together. Two frosty females resenting each other. I confessed how I'd often wished it had been mum who died in the crash, and how I hated myself for thinking such a wicked thing.

Mum, finally in pole-position had taken authority to a new level. She became like an overbearing shadow that influenced every part of my life. I admitted how I grew to hate her, but never had the guts to say 'no' to her. I explain how mum had railroaded me into marrying Mark, who she thought was the perfect catch.

I brush over how Mark had made me feel ugly and unwanted, and that brief admission brings a deluge of tears.

Maria passes me a tissue and remains quiet until my tears subside.

'I'm so sorry,' I stutter, wiping my face. 'I shouldn't have told you all that about Mark. He's honestly a decent man, very caring. He didn't mean to hurt me.'

'Nor did your mother.'

I sink back in my chair; I don't think I want to hear what Maria has to say anymore.

'No one ever has reached perfezione, you comprendere, mia dolce ragazza.' While speaking Maria has gripped two fingers and thumbs on the tips and is waving her hand at me.

I nod, but I want to leave.

'When you become momma, you h'are madre per sempre. You cannot undo what you 'av become.' She leans forward and reaches for my hand. I reach over and take it. She nods. Now I'm convinced she is the wisest woman in the world. I sit forward. I want to learn, to grow.

She smiles. Skin crinkles around her eyes. She pats my hand. 'Once you are momma, you never stop worrying about your figli until the day you die. It is *impossibile* to stop. Love'a makes us crazy!' With one hand she flicks the side of her head. 'Totalmente pazzo!'

I'm not a hundred per cent sure what that means, but I take a guess at totally crazy.

'Be kind to the memory of your momma, from what you 'ave said I can see that she loved molto!' Molto is said forcefully, it brings a lump to my throat. I know mum loved me. My issue was always that I didn't think I loved her. I put the wall up between us every time I pushed her away only wanting my dad. Remorse washes over me like a tsunami, before I can take a breath I am sobbing again.

Maria pulls me onto her chest and pats my back, and strokes my hair. I sob. Pain flows from me and dissipates into the air.

'Ragazza dolce,' she whispers in between kissing my hair.

Gratitude and affection for this old woman, who I hardly know, is like a refreshing shower. I feel washed, calmed, and restored.

When I'm finished I sit back and mumble thanks.

'Pass me please, the rosary on the writing desk.'

I get up and cross the room. Lying on the desk is a rosary bead string, with a simple silver cross. I hand it to her.

She asks for my hand, and then puts the rosary in my palm and closes my fingers around it.

'Oh, I couldn't take it.'

'Sì, it h'is for you, I got it ready for you.'

'You planned to give it to me?' Had she known I was on the edge?

'You will pray, ask'a God to forgive you, your mother and this stupido husband of yours.'

'Oh, I don't pray.' I try giving it back, she sits back. 'Please, I don't believe in God, there's no point me having it.'

'Then you will'a take it if only to please me, no?'

'OK.'

'Now go back to your painting and lovely music, enjoy your holiday.'

'Thank you, I'll try.'

We kiss, three times on each cheek, but as I'm leaning back she grabs my wrist and stares right into my eyes. A certain 'glint' in her eyes hints of the seriousness of her next words.

'And you will'a stay away'a from Giovanni, no? He needs a nice'a woman, one who will'a love him.'

It's a sour end to what had just been a revelation to me, but she's right.

I nod.

I can't give Gio anything. If I said I only wanted to be friends with benefits I would be lying. I'm too confused to explain anything. The easiest thing to do would be to simply stop seeing him.

But I don't think I can do that.

Chapter 24

Giovanni – Something in the Way She Moves

MY FATHER IS WATCHING my every move. I feel like an animal in a zoo, and very uncomfortable. I close the window and use the control to turn on the air conditioning.

'You OK there son?'

'Yes, Papà.'

We work in silence for a little while, then he puts down his pen with a deliberate tap so that I look up at him.

'What's going on Giovanni?'

Full name, that's somber stuff. 'Shall we get coffee?'

He nods. I don't spend enough time with my folks, I wish I did. We're a very close-knit family, but living in London means I miss out on a lot. When I am here though, working with him renews our bond making it as firm as ever. Coffee on the balcony is our go-to thing when we want a chat.

We both choose to stand on the veranda, next to the balustrade, looking out to sea. The view from my family home is amazing and I never get tired of it. I am reminded how lucky we are.

'So, you were going to take the week off?'

'I know, change of plan. I might take a couple of days off next week instead.'

'What happened son?'

I have this awful feeling that I'm about to sound like an adolescent boy.

'How did you know when you were in love with Momma?'

He turns his head sharply to look at me. 'That serious, huh?'

'Yeah, I think it is.'

'I think I loved momma from the first time I saw her. I couldn't take my eyes off her; there was something in the way she moved that hypnotized me. I wasn't sure it was love at first, but then one day my friend Peter started talking to her. I was so jealous I wanted to punch him.'

Papà laughs. 'I later found out momma hates violence, can you imagine her response if I had lashed out?'

'Did she love you straight away?'

'No, not at all,' he laughs again. 'She played hard to get for a very long time. I don't think she could make her mind up. She told me later that she didn't want to be a traditional wife and momma, she wanted more.'

'I didn't know that.' But it explains why I spent so much of my childhood with Nonna. 'What did you tell her?'

'I told her that whatever her dreams were, I would make them come true.'

'What did she say?'

'That she wanted to make her dreams come true herself!'

I laugh. 'Sounds just like Momma.'

Papà chuckles.

'So that's why you work together.'

'We were lucky my parents started the business, they were more than happy for us to work with them. Over time we all found the things that we excelled in and the Lord blessed us as a team.' He smiles at me. I know it pleases him that I want to stay in the family business.

Lorenzo and Francesco built a new company together and now own a casino chain that makes them piles of money. Sofia works in our company, but she's not as committed as me and hasn't found that thing that gives her a lot of satisfaction yet.

'Tell me about this woman that has you in a spin.'

'I've only known her a week.'

'That doesn't matter, tell me what you know.'

What do I know? 'She's feisty and I have to tread carefully. She's beautiful and has stunning red hair. She loves the sea like me, we like a lot of the same things. When I'm with her I feel comfortable and excited at the same time. We've talked for hours and I know lots about her...' How can I sum her up?

'She makes my heart race, and fills my nights with dreams about her. I love to watch her move. She's graceful like a gazelle, and comfortable in her own skin. She hardly wears make up and doesn't seem to care too much about what people think of her.'

'She sounds lovely. What's her name?

'Selene.'

'Selene, Titan goddess from Greek mythology, daughter of Hyperion and Theia. Her brother, Helios, is the god of the sun, and her sister, Eos, is the goddess of the dawn.'

'How do you know that?'

'We learned it at college, but I remember it because we almost called Sofia, Selene.'

'Huh, small world. I'm glad you changed your mind, it would make things odd being in love with someone with the same name as my sister.'

'You're in love?'

We turn from the view of the sea to look at each other.

'I think I am.'

'Then do everything you can to win her heart, son.'

Chapter 25

Selene – Step into my Web said the Spider

I'VE NEVER BEEN INTO SQUEALS but when Shelley's car pulls up outside on Thursday evening, I feel like a school kid and jump and flap my arms. We squeal, we hug and then I help her take her bags into the cottage.

'Geez, Shelley, what have you got here? You've only come for three nights *haven't you*?' The 'haven't you' raised a pitch at the thought that she might have invited herself for a longer stay.

'I had to be sure to bring everything I *might* need.' She winks at me.

'I thought we were just going to relax, go on long walks, spend the day at the beach, things like that.'

'Oh,' she flaps her hands at me, 'of course we'll do those things. But we'll be going out in the evenings and I want to be prepared. I might meet the man of my dreams here, you never know. And you said Giovanni has two brothers, right?'

'I don't know much about them. One of them is married anyway.' I'm a little crushed. I'd been daydreaming of a girlie weekend, chillaxing and having fun. Nowhere in my plans was the thought that Shelley would be introduced to Gio, or that we would be going out at night looking for men. Silly me though, I should have known. This is my best friend through and through. My party animal who thrives on fun.

My phone pings, it's Gio. I wonder if he'd been waiting to see Shelley's car arrive.

Gio sent: *Hey Bella, would you and Shelley like to join me and some friends at Da Casa a Casa tomorrow for dinner? xx*

I read the text to Shelley. She jumps up and claps her hands. 'Oh, yeah! Let's go. I can't wait to meet the Italian Stallion!'

I cringe at her words. I don't think of Gio like that anymore. She clearly notes my worried face and misinterprets it.

'Hey, it's up to you of course. If you're ashamed of me, then of course we won't go.'

'Don't be silly! I'm *not* ashamed of you.'

'Then why wouldn't you want us to meet?'

'I don't think of him as a summer-fling anymore Shelley, but I don't want him to know that. I wanted to spend time telling you everything, but if you're going to see him, well I, I…' I just don't know how to verbalize my fears.

'Hey, it's not a problem. If you don't want to go, we'll stay here and have a pajama party!'

I love Shelley. She's been a true friend for years. I know she wants to go out and have some fun.

I text back: *Meet you there, what time? x*

He types back immediately: *Love that I've finally got a text kiss XX We'll be there at eight. xxxx*

I laugh as I send back just an emoji face with a heart on its mouth.

'Looks like we're going out for a meal tomorrow night,' I grin.

'Yeah!' shrieks Shelley jumping up and hugging me.

We spend the rest of the night catching up on all our news. We try to watch a movie but end up chatting all the way through it.

After breakfast we head into Torquay, officially for sightseeing but mainly for shopping. We eat lunch on the waterfront and afterwards go for a leisurely walk along the beach.

'This place is amazing,' says Shelley.

I have to agree with her.

'BEST START GETTING READY. We've got an hour and a half.'

'Whoop-whoop!'

We gab non-stop as we get ready. I can't believe that Shelley has brought ten different pairs of high heels with her, it gives me the giggles. That and the sparkling wine she insists we drink as we get ready. I honestly don't put up much resistance!

I put on a new outfit that I purchased yesterday. The palazzo trousers are magenta pink, and the top a very pale (almost see-through) pink. I put on new lingerie that I purchased at the same time. It's a deep red with black lace. I've never owned anything so sexy in my life – but that's how Giovanni is changing me. I'm looking at the world with new eyes, and I like what I see.

I decided to go all out with the makeup. Shelley's an expert at it, so I let her contour my cheeks and put on smoky eye shadow and dark brown eyeliner. By the time I've put my lipstick on, I can hardly recognize myself.

'Wow!' she says. 'You're a knock-out today, girl!'

I look at myself in the full-length mirror, something I very rarely do. It's a 'good' day and I'm pleased with the look I've accomplished.

I know it's wrong, *really wrong*, to want Gio to want me when I'm planning on walking away in a few weeks. But I do. Desire rises from my feet to my head, heating all the intimate parts of my body. I'm practically pulsating with lust. When Shelley is in the bathroom, I step closer to the mirror.

'Come into my web, said the spider to the fly,' I say under my breath.

I want to catch him. I want him to want me. I want to be naughty, and I want to have fun. I'm attracted to more than his appearance, but I'm trying to convince myself a holiday romance is still all that I want.

Shelley comes out of the bathroom looking spectacular. She's in a yellow dress which clings to her body in all the right places. It's very sexy. She's got on six-inch high-heeled shoes. Around her neck adding color, is a necklace of bright colored beads. She's pinned her hair up and done her makeup similar to mine, she's simply divine.

'You didn't hold back then,' I laugh.

'No chance, baby!'

I've booked us an Uber and not long after we're ready it beeps its horn outside. I half expected Gio to offer to pick us up, but I'm glad he didn't. Going with Shelley in a taxi like this feels more natural.

I wasn't expecting the restaurant to be packed, as the last time I came it had been quiet. Tonight the place is heaving. Pop music is playing and the atmosphere is lively and fun. It is nothing like the first time I came, and I wonder if it's because it had been a Sunday and there hadn't been any music.

Gio stands up as soon we walk in. He comes over to us. Damn, but he's hot! I can't believe it has been less than three days since we've seen each other, it feels so long ago.

He kisses me on both cheeks. 'Bella, you look amazing,' he says quietly.

'Gio this is Shelley. Shelley this is Gio.'

'Ciao, lovely to meet you,' says Giovanni.

'Likewise,' says Shelley moving in for a kiss-cheek. 'Very continental,' she winks at me as we walk across the restaurant.

'Let me introduce you. Everyone this is Selene and Shelley.' A chorus of hi's and hello's is raised.

Gio introduces us to everyone at the table. 'John and Mike you know. This is Danni and Susan.' He points to a handsome guy that just has to be one of his brothers. 'This is Francesco, my brother.'

Francesco stands and reaches across the table to shake hands. 'A pleasure to meet you,' he says shaking my hand. By his smile I can deduce that he knows all about me.

'Lastly, we have Mary and Joseph.'

I can't help smiling.

'I know,' says Joseph standing up to shake my hand. 'I have no idea what our parents were thinking. We've been the butt of jokes all our lives.'

'Nice to meet you,' I say.

Introductions done we sit down at the very large circular table.

Everyone starts talking again at the same time. I feel nervous all of a sudden. I hadn't expected to meet his brother; suddenly it matters to me that he approves of me. Gio drops a hand onto my thigh and gives me a reassuring squeeze.

Luckily for me, Shelley loves being the center of attention and soon the majority of the focus is on her. I give a happy sigh. Gio leans in and kisses my cheek. I turn to smile at him. Happiness oozes off him, it infects me and I feel a bubble of joy rising.

The meal is a huge success. We all laugh and share stories all night. Everyone seems eager to share every embarrassing moment that Giovanni has ever had, and some things are hilarious.

When we say goodbye at the end of the evening I'm a little sad I'm not taking Gio back with me. We stand in the car park waiting for the Uber. He is behind me and has his arms wrapped around me. Waves of comfort envelop me.

My phone pings to say the taxi is two minutes away.

'Ladies, my folks are throwing a birthday party for my grandmother tomorrow. You've both been invited. I hope you'll come.'

'Oh no, I don't think so.'

'Of course we'll come. I'd love to meet your family Gio, if they're anything like you and Francesco then I already know they're lovely people!'

'Great. It starts at one at my parent's house. I'll come and pick you up if you like?'

He's trying to let me know I'm still in control because he's only looking at me when he asks that.

'We'll grab a taxi, just text me the address.'

'Will do.'

I feel pushed into doing something I don't want. All sorts of anger issues rise in my chest. Not at anyone else, at myself for not saying no.

Before I close the taxi door, I lean back out. 'Gio, what can we buy your grandmother as a present.'

'She's not big on presents, Selene. The only thing she ever asks for is our presence to celebrate with her.'

We both wave out of the back window as we drive away.

'Selene, that man is a keeper. You can't let him go! Please say you're going to marry him and have his babies.'

I am changing. I will change. I will start right now.

'No.'

Chapter 26

Giovanni – Family is Everything

PUTTING MY HANDS behind my head, I stretch out on the sofa, more relaxed than I've been in years.

'Momma, I've got this odd feeling here,' I thump my chest, 'when I'm with her.'

Her thick dark eyebrows shoot up, 'Love?'

'Maybe.'

'Tell me what you're feeling, mio piccolo Bambino?'

'I can't explain it, but being with her makes me feel good.'

Momma and Sofia throw glances at each other.

'Sounds like you're happy to me,' says Sofia with a sparkle in her eye.

I know they think I'm falling in love, but I don't want their exuberance to scare off Selene or give them false hope for my future. I might be feeling things I've never felt before, but I know Selene isn't. 'You know what it is, it's like I can just be myself when I'm with her. I don't have to pretend anything. And I don't have to constantly check if she's OK. She just is. She's always so calm, yet deep and …'

There's a roar of laughter. When I've been happily ceiling gazing, Papà and Francesco have turned up in the living room. The four of them are having a jolly old laugh at my expense.

I roll my eyes. 'What?' I say sitting up.

'Oh, Bambino, you got it bad,' Momma laughs.

'Never thought I'd see the day,' says Francesco.

Standing up, I raise my shoulders and arms in the classic 'so what' gesture.

'Come on Gio, you can't deny us our fun, this has been years in the making,' laughs Francesco making a heart shape with his hands and pressing it against his chest.

'What fun is that?' asks Lorenzo coming in with his wife Karen, and their two boys Harry and Joe.

'Don't we have a party to prepare?' I ask trying to deflect.

'Everything is ready,' says Momma.

Of course it is!

'Gio's is love,' Francesco tells Lorenzo.

'Good Lord! Really?' asks Karen. 'Never thought I'd see the day.'

'I'm going to pick up Nonna.'

They're all ribbing me and calling out daft things as I head out. I only popped over early without Nonna to make sure Momma didn't need any help. Of course I should have known everything would be fully ready. I know they'll all be talking about Selene now, and pumping Francesco for details about her. Not that he can say that much as he's only met her once, still... it's giving me a headache.

By the time I get back with Nonna, the forecourt is full of cars. Fairy lights have been laced between all the trees and the buildings, and although it's still daytime it's overcast and the lights can just be seen.

'Spreco di energia elettrica,' grumbles Nonna.

'One afternoon won't hurt, Nonna. It's not like we have lights like this all year round.'

Nonna has always been a feisty woman and very vocal, but today she seems a little down, her words more brittle than normal.

I offer her my arm. 'Forza mia bella principessa, ti portiamo al ballo!'

She tuts, but wraps her arm through mine.

As soon as we walk in everyone starts singing happy birthday. Nonna stands and smiles at her loved ones, and friends of the family. When they finish singing, there is a rush to come and kiss and hug. I leave her to it, as my eyes search for Selene.

'She's not here yet, Gio.' Sofia comes and stands next to me. 'Do you think she changed her mind?'

I check my phone. There's no new text from her. 'I don't think so, I think she would have let me know if that was the case.'

'She's probably as nervous as fuck!'

'Sofia!' snaps Momma who was just walking by.

'Mi scusi,' Sofia replies, pulling a face at me while rolling her eyes.

'Don't roll your eyes at me, figlia!'

I can't help but laugh. Momma is walking away and couldn't see Sofia's face, the comment comes from knowing her daughter well.

'Gio!' Sofia has grabbed my arm.

I turn to look out the window. A taxi is coming up the drive.

We both head to the door. We're quickly followed by Papà, Lorenzo and Francesco.

'Too much!' I say as I open the door, but none of them back away. Family!

I head down the steps to help Selene out of the car. A pile of Italian expletives fires off in my mind. She could be a movie star. She's in a long, summer dress. It's a white fabric with splashes of deep red, the halter-neck is loose and swishes when she moves, but clings to all the right places. It's the first time I've seen her in really high heels, they add height and elegance to her voluptuous curves. She's fully made-up and her eyes are striking. Her hair is pinned in loose waves on the top of her head.

She takes my hand. We wait for Shelley to come around the taxi and then we turn to face my family.

I groan. Momma, Karen, Harry, and Joe have joined the others standing on the steps.

Momma can't wait for us to reach the door. She flies down the steps.

'Sorry,' I say.

Selene is half-turning to ask me what for when Momma engulfs her in a hug. Kisses and hugs and more kisses.

'Welcome, welcome,' she says. I can tell she doesn't want to let Selene go, but she's a thoughtful host so she does and moves on to kiss Shelley.

'That's my mother, Fiorella.'

Luckily, most of the others either just nod or offer to shake hands. Papà claims a three-cheek-kiss exchange. 'Arturo, sei il benvenuto a casa nostra.'

'Thank you for inviting us, Arturo.'

As we walk in I whisper to Selene, 'Sorry about that.'

She squeezes my hand, 'You have nothing to be sorry about. Your family are lovely, and that was very welcoming.'

We go through the house and out into the garden, where (weather permitting) we will spend the day.

'Where's Maria?' asks Selene.

'Over there, under the gazebo.'

'I'd like to wish her happy birthday.'

'Sure, you guys go and do that and then come and find me.'

Chapter 27

Selene – A Real Famiglia

'HAPPY BIRTHDAY, MARIA.' I'm relieved when she smiles up at me and pats the chair next to her. I wasn't too sure she'd be happy to see me here.

'Sedersi,' she says, and Shelley and I take seats on either side of her.

'Giovanni told me that you don't really want presents, but I hope you won't mind that I have got a little something for you. It's from both of us.' I nod towards Shelley, and pass a little gift-wrapped box that we purchased this morning on a hasty re-visit to Torquay.

'I can't take things with me to Heaven, and I'm going soon, so presents are a waste of money.' Although she grumbles I think I see a slight excitement in her as she unwraps the box.

When she lifts the lid and sees the butterfly broach she 'Ooohs.' It is obvious she likes it, and I'm so glad I didn't listen to Gio.

'Help me?' she asks, and I go to pin the broach on the shoulder of her dress.

'No, no, not there, here.' She points to the center of her v-neckline. It seems quite provocative to put it there, but she insists. I get an image in my mind of what she must have been like in her younger years and believe she must have been a lot of fun.

She puts her hands up to hold my face, and we kiss cheeks again. 'Tante grazie.'

'You're welcome.'

'Now introduce me to you beautiful friend.'

'This is Shelley, Shelley this is Maria.'

They kiss.

'Tell me Shelley… are you single?'

Shelley laughs. 'Unfortunately, yes.'

Maria pats her hand and winks at her. 'Maybe not for long, you know my grandson is still single.'

I choke on nothing. Is she trying to pair Shelley and Gio together?

She's grinning at me, and immediately I see the humor in her eyes. Crafty old thing!

'Ladies, I brought you some drinks.' Gio has arrived with a tray of glasses.

'Thank you,' I say lifting a glass of rosé.

Shelley takes a glass and Gio passes Maria, a tall glass with what looks like homemade lemonade in it. I smile as she takes it and wonder if it really is homemade.

One-by-one all the family and other guests start joining us under the gazebo, we sit in a circle and Maria is definitely the center of attention. I love the family interaction and the ease in which they all talk. Now and again the conversation drifts into Italian but someone always brings it back to English pretty quickly. It's inclusive and it's lovely.

I notice that Lorenzo's taken the seat next to Shelley and has been talking mainly with her since he sat down. She's beaming from ear to ear. Yesterday, she'd told me how much she's found Lorenzo attractive but that he seemed too rich and handsome to have any interest in her. It seems she might have been wrong on that score.

Maria taps my hand and I look at her. She nods towards Shelley and Lorenzo and winks, and I suddenly realize she meant Lorenzo when she said her grandson was single. How could she possibly have known that he would like her?

'I need to go and check that dinner is ready to start. Come with me?' Sofia asks me. It would be rude to say no, so I say, 'Sure,' and go with her. As we're walking across the massive lawn towards the house, I blurt out a question.

'I think your grandmother knew that Lorenzo would like Shelley, how could she have guessed? Does he have a type or something?'

Sofia burst out laughing. 'No he doesn't have a type. Nonna would know because *everyone* tells her *everything*. That makes her the font of all knowledge. We all have a close relationship with her. Lorenzo probably visited her yesterday and told her all about the meal on Friday night.'

'Oh, that makes sense.' And wow… that means he must have taken an instant liking to her, wow, I never saw that coming.

'Do Italian men tell their grandmothers everything?'

Sofia laughs again and links her arm through mine. 'You have so much to learn. It would be my pleasure to teach you. Yes, if they have a close relationship, Italian men tell their grandmothers everything.'

'Does Giovanni have a close relationship with Maria?'

'Very.'

'Oh.' I'm not sure I like the thought of him telling her what we've been up to.

'What you have to understand is that English men and Italian men are two completely different species. English men wait patiently in queues, Italian men drive scooters up to the front of the line, and where you might get irritated, they wave and say ciao baby, and voilà you're not cross anymore.'

I chuckle, I can't help it, the image sums up the pieces of Italian culture I've picked up from movies and books. 'I can't see Gio on a scooter though,' I laugh.

'Women say arrivederci and English men walk away with their tails between their legs. But Italian men, oh la la…' Sofia flaps her hand in front of her. 'Italian men don't let go, they fight for their woman, they think that once they love, then they love forever.'

'That sounds very passionate.'

As we enter the house through open patio doors, Sofia says, 'All Italian men are passionate, Italian women are lucky, no?'

'They are!' I'm smiling, but inside chaos is forming. Is she letting me know that she knows Giovanni loves me and that he won't give up without a fight when I leave?

Sofia lets go of my arm and has a discussion in Italian with a female cook. She turns back to me smiling.

'We're all set. Let's tell the others.'

Instead of walking all the way across the lawn again, Sofia picks up a brass bell from a kitchen shelf, she walks outside onto the patio and rings the bell.

I laugh, 'Do you always call everyone to dinner like that?'

'Momma did when we were children. We would be scattered all over the grounds, so she rang the bell. It was easier than looking for us.'

'Good idea.'

Along the back of the house is a huge patio area. Overhead is a grand pagoda that runs the whole length of the building. Growing up and over it are a variety of clematis and honeysuckle. It's a spread of pinks and purples and is just lovely.

A long wooden table has been set in the center and everyone begins to take their seats.

Shelley and I hesitate not sure where to sit.

'You're next to me,' Francesco tells Shelley and leads her away.

'This way,' says Gio, who guides us to the top end of the table next to his father. 'He wants to get to know you,' he whispers in my ear as I sit in the chair he's just pulled out for me.

From the moment we sit it's an explosion of discussion and laughter. Waiters appear and start pouring wine for everyone. Waitresses flood from the kitchen with platters of antipasto. Pickles and grissini are already on the table. Everyone helps themselves, but no one eats. I put some delicious salami and prosciutto ham on my plate but wait to see what we're doing.

When everyone has food on their plate, Arturo stands up and clinks an empty glass with a spoon. Quiet descends.

'Thank you, friends both old and new, for joining us on this special day. Nonna, we are here to celebrate your life with you. We would be nothing without you. Our thanks to you and Nonno flow from our hearts today, as they did yesterday and as they will tomorrow. We are family, and you are our heart. Buon compleanno Momma, we love you!'

'Saluti' and 'buon compleanno' chorus around. Lots of cheers go up and some people bang their glasses on the table.

Maria, who is sitting at the end of the table on the other side, waves a hand for everyone to stop. She places a hand over her heart. 'You are'a my life,' she says. Then she waves her hands. 'Now eat, before you all end up drunk!'

After Arturo has eaten a little, I lean towards him slightly. 'That was a lovely speech.'

'The short ones are the best!' he laughs.

I laugh along; he knows that's not what I meant.

'Tell me a little about you,' he says.

In between delicious mouthfuls of antipasto I tell him a little of myself, where I went to college things like that. By the time we move onto the pasta course I'm very much at ease with him. Arturo is like a mature Giovanni, and I can imagine that Gio will end up like this relaxed and gentle man.

By the time we are being served the secondo, which is a flamed grilled steak, I start to talk to the other family members. They have me laughing so much that it is hard to eat. Our wine glasses are continually filled. I notice everyone alternates between their wine and water glass and I start doing the same. It's only three in the afternoon and I don't want to embarrass myself by getting drunk.

'I tell you it's true,' says Karen.

'And that is coming from a non-Italian,' adds Lorenzo leaning across the table and waving his fork at me.

'Mixing meats gives you indigestion!' Karen confirms.

Francesco waves his hand at me. 'And don't get us started on meatballs!'

Arturo goes off into Italian that I don't understand; he seems angry and is waving his hands about.

Gio grins at me. 'It's true… Italians don't eat meatballs on pasta. That's a meal created by Disney's Lady and the Tramp.'

'Is it?' I know my eyes are wide. 'I always thought that was a popular Italian dish.'

All the Italians on the table, and Karen, go off into a rant waving their hands and biting their knuckles. The noise makes me sit back a little.

Then they're laughing. Arturo puts a hand on my shoulder. 'You'll get used to us noisy Italians,' he laughs.

'Dolce! Torta alla Panna,' announces a waiter, approaching the table with a massive cake on a silver platter balanced on his shoulder.

Everyone claps. He places it in front of Maria, but she's ordering the waiter something in Italian.

'She says she's too old to serve everyone, which is our tradition. Momma is going to do it instead.' Sure enough, the waiter picks up the silver tray and brings the strawberry topped cake to place in front of Fiorella.

Gio's hand rests on my thigh under the table. It's the first intimate contact we've had since I arrived. I think the both of us have finally relaxed in front of his family.

As I watch Fiorella slice the cake and put it on plates that are passed along the table, I get family envy. My family, even when my parents were alive, was so small. I would have loved a large family like this.

With the arrival of the cake, two things happen. The waitresses bring us flutes and bottles and bottles of Champagne, and a trio of guitar-playing singers, walk out of the house and start serenading us with Italian songs. Most people at the table start singing along.

I've never heard any of the songs before, but they're lively and fun.

As soon as the dessert plates are cleared away, a waiter comes around with a trolley filled with different digestifs including Amaro and Montengro.

'Try the Amaro,' says Gio, 'you'll love it.'

'I don't think I had better mix any more alcohol, I'll topple over.'

Arturo heard me and indicates for the waiter to serve me some Amaro. 'You need to digest the food, it is very important.'

'OK, thank you.' One of these days I *will* learn how to say no, but not today, because I'm having such a lovely time.

Chapter 28

Giovanni – Shall we Dance?

'UN VERO ITALIANO!' Once someone called it out, everyone joins in. Baptism by fire, I think, as I take in Selene's amused face as people start pulling me out of my seat.

'Sorry!' I laugh as they drag me off. 'It's a family tradition, you have to forgive us!'

My brothers and Papà join me. Papà is passed a tambourine, the guitarists start playing 'un vero Italiano' which means just one Italian. The four of us start singing. After the first verse everyone, including the band, joins in.

It's loud. We sing it with all our might. The women clap, Selene and Shelley join them. My eyes hardly leave hers. Every now and again I look at Nonna, who is singing and clapping, but then like a magnet I'm drawn back to Selene. I love that she's joining in. My cup overflows, as they say.

When we finish there are cries to repeat, but I think once is enough for Selene for the first time. As I'm walking back to her, happiness radiates off me. This is one of those perfect days. One I will store in my heart forever. The first time Selene joined us for a family meal. Please (to all the powers that be) this is the first of a thousand.

The liveliness continues for a while with lots of clapping and singing along with the guitarists. When they

173

leave, Papà gets up and puts his favorite LP on the record player. Speakers are permanently placed at either side of the patio. As soon as the music starts, momma stands up and goes around the table. This is their song. They dance it at every party without fail. *Dance me to the end of love* by *Leonard Cohen*.

We let them have the floor to themselves for the first verse and then we start joining in. I would normally dance with Nonna, but my uncle nods at me indicating that he will keep her company for this dance.

I offer Selene my hand and immediately pull her into my chest. I place my left hand in the small of her back and press to keep her close to me. She places her small hand in my right hand and I waltz her slowly over the tiles. Every part of my body is alive. *My friend* is instantly awake. I persuade him now is not the time. Selene is like a doll in my hands, where I turn and lead us she sways with ease.

I breathe deep the wafts of vanilla and musk rising from her neck. I don't think of my parents waltzing by beside us. I lean in and kiss her neck. She shivers in my arms. I think it might be best if we had some alone time, the cottage won't work because Shelley will be there. Thinking about Selene's friend makes me lift my head to check she is OK. She's in Francesco's arms; her head is on his chest. He winks at me over her head as he moves her around. As the album moves into the second song, which is *A Thousand Kisses Deep*, everyone continues dancing.

Selene must sense I'm looking around because she looks up at me. Her green eyes are sexy as hell and lusty and I know what she's thinking. I maneuver us slowly across the tiles until we're next to Francesco and Shelley.

'Hey guys, what are you thinking of doing next?'

Francesco turns his attention to Shelley, who nods at him. 'As it happens, we're going to the waterfront. Shelley would like to see my yacht.'

Selene startles in my arms. 'Really?' she says and I can tell she doesn't think it's a good idea.

'You're welcome to come too, of course,' says Francesco. Shelley frowns at Selene. She obviously doesn't want company.

'No, it's OK, I think I've had a bit too much to drink, I think I'll get a taxi and go home.'

Shelley grins. 'Lightweight!' she laughs.

'Excuse me,' says Papà. 'May I?'

I grin. 'You and me, Momma!' Momma laughs and I whirl off round and round as we dance away, leaving Papà to dance with Selene. I can't help but throw constant glances her way, I'm always worried about her.

'This one is special, aye.'

I look at Momma, who is beaming from ear to ear.

'Yes Momma, this is *the one*.'

'About time,' she laughs. 'I'd like grandchildren before I'm too old to play with them.'

'You already have grandchildren, Momma.'

She laughs. 'Well, I'm greedy!'

Getting out of the house takes some time as everyone wants to kiss Selene goodbye and have a chat with her. Eventually, we're climbing into an Uber.

I don't ask if I can come back with her, I know she wants me just as much as I want her. She sinks against my chest. I wrap my arm around her and will the taxi to break the speed limit.

'Do you think Shelley will be alright?' she asks once we're inside the cottage.

'Yes of course, my brother's not a cad.'

'I know, but they've only just met.'

'He's only showing off his boat, it's his pride and joy. You don't have to worry… I promise.'

'Can we dance again?'

'What do you have in mind?'

'Do you have 'dance me to the end of love' on your playlist?'

'Indeed I do.'

I connect my phone to Selene's Bluetooth speaker and Leonard's husky voice fills the room.

I offer my hand. She takes it. I spin her under my arm and then pull her into my chest, immediately we're slow waltzing around the kitchen table. She places her head on my shoulder. This time I don't need to have words with *my friend* when he flicks to life. I press the hardness of him against Selene. She sucks in her breath and tightens her grip around my neck.

I dance us into the bedroom.

We kick off our shoes but don't stop dancing. Turn, spin, one-two-three, one-two-three, turn. I lean back and start undoing my shirt buttons. Selene takes off her earrings and drops them on the dresser.

I put my shirt on the back of the chair and turn around to see Selene kicking her undies across the room. The thought that under that dress is nothing urges me to grab her. I place my hand on the back of her head and we return to the waltz. One-two-three, one-two-three, spin, repeat. She's running her nails up and down my bare chest. Thrills race over me.

I kiss her neck. She moans.

I start pulling up her dress until my hand can find the top of her legs. She leans into me, I have to push her back a little to work my magic. She's groaning. I pick her up. She wraps her legs around my waist.

'There's something in the way,' she murmurs.

'Not for long.'

I continue dancing with her in my arm. She's plastering my neck and chest with kisses. One-two-three, one-two-three, spin. I drop her onto the bed. My trousers are off and on the floor. I don't pick them up.

I push up her dress and climb over her. I've been waiting all day for this, I'll play later. For now I have to claim her. I push. She yields.

In and out – back and forth. Leonard sings, we move. One-two, one-two, one-two.

Perfect day.

Perfect woman.

Perfect moment.

The alcohol and delightful exercise send us both off to sleep. It's dark when I wake. Selene is still asleep with her head on my chest. Neither of us has moved since we drifted off.

I don't want to disturb the moment, but nature is calling. I try to carefully lift my arm out from under her. My arm is dead; I can't help the groan I give. She's awake instantly and moves out of the way.

'I'm sorry, I must have crushed you.'

'Not at all, I've just got a bit of cramp that's all.'

After using the bathroom and washing my hands for exactly three minutes I come out with a towel wrapped around my waist.

'Suits you,' she grins.

'Thanks, I thought I'd start a new craze. I'm getting some water, would you like some.'

'Yes please.'

When I come back, Selene is washing in the bathroom. She comes out with a towel wrapped around her. 'Matching outfits,' she laughs and hops onto the bed beside me.

After we've had a drink we lie back down.

'Shelley's not back yet.'

'No. Hey, I promise you she will be OK. Have you checked your phone to see if she has texted you?'

'Yep, she sent a photo of her and Francesco on the boat, pretty impressive.'

'I promise my brother is a gentleman, she's in safe hands.'

Selene sighs.

I lie on my side and start kissing her shoulder. I must tickle her because she gets the giggles. I kiss her neck and jawline. The giggles are gone and now she sighs.

A deluge of emotions sweeps over me. Unfortunately, it means I go to speak before I think.

'Selene,' I say in between kisses.

'Umm.'

'I lo…'

'Don't say it!' She bolts upright and stares at me. 'DON'T SAY IT!'

I feel heat flood my cheeks. I'm not only embarrassed but hate being told what to do.

'Say what?' I snap.

'You know what.'

'Do I?'

Her breathing has become rapid. She's wound up tight.

'Why not?' I ask when she doesn't answer.

'Because I'm on holiday, this,' she flaps her hand between us, 'this… is just a holiday thing, nothing more. At the end of it I'm leaving.'

'Would it really be so bad if we fell in love?' I feel crushed and confused because every inch of her body tells me that she loves me too.

'That wouldn't be so bad, what would be terrible though, is if one of us fell in love and the other one didn't.'

I don't believe her. She loves me I know she does. Merda! What do I do?

She gets out of bed and puts her dressing gown on. 'I think you should go.'

It's cold, it's brutal, and I'm not staying around to be insulted.

I dress in silence. When I'm ready to leave she stands in the kitchen and doesn't come near me. Very well, I'm not begging.

I slam the door behind me.

Chapter 29

Selene – Planning

SHELLEY DOESN'T COME BACK until eleven o'clock the following morning. I hear a car outside and open the door. The two of them are in an embrace that tells me all I need to know. I go back inside, leaving the door open.

'Hey you!' Shelley says as she comes bouncing in. Her smile is wide and her eyes are glistening. She's undoubtedly had fun. I try to crush the irritation that's popping inside me.

'Hi, did you have a good time?'

'The best! Oh my goodness, you should see his yacht, it's beautiful and so elegant. I felt like Jackie Onassis on there.' She laughs as she flops down on the sofa.

'I'm glad you enjoyed yourself.' I hope I sound sincere because I can't help thinking of all the complications that might arise from this. One of the biggest being, if they start a relationship and she ends up moving down here, how will I be able to avoid Giovanni in the future?

'You cross at me?'

I sigh and sit on a chair near her. 'No. I was a bit worried about you though.'

'You needn't have been. I had the best time!'

'Would you like a cup of tea?'

'Love one, thanks.'

I go and put the kettle on and get cups and milk out. Shelley follows me and hovers around the table.

'I had a great time.'

'You said.'

'No, Selene, I mean I had a really *great* time.'

I can't help laughing. 'I can tell. Go on then, tell me all about it.'

Bubbling over with excitement, Shelley tells me about their passionate night and about their breakfast in bed. It all sounded very *Hollywood* to me.

'What happens now?' I ask.

'Nothing of course.'

'What do you mean?' I pass her a cup of tea.

She takes a sip and then leans her head to one side and gives me that *really* look.

'I mean nothing. Nothing is going to happen now. It was one night of absolute pleasure that's all.'

'You don't want to see him again?'

Shelley sighs and pulls out a kitchen chair. I do the same and we sit down.

'You know they're all billionaires don't you?'

'What?' No I didn't, the news gave me a jolt. How did I not know that?

'Haven't you Googled them yet?'

'No. Gio told me he wasn't on social media, so I've not looked.'

'I don't mean social media, I mean the news etc. The Giacomelli Corporation is ranked ninety-two in the Top 500 Fortune List.'

'That's like off-the-scale rich, right?'

'Right.'

'I didn't know.'

'Girl you walk around with your head in the clouds. You've got to get into the habit of researching anyone you're thinking of dating. I mean you need to make sure they haven't got a criminal record for a start. The world's not a safe place anymore; you've got to take precautions.'

'I wasn't looking for a boyfriend, and this thing between Giovanni and I will finish the day I drive away from Cockington.'

'Are you sure?'

'Positive.'

'But you seem made for each other, everyone thinks so.'

'Everyone?'

'Yeah, I probably shouldn't tell you but Francesco said they're all taking bets that you'll be married within a year.'

I feel sick. 'That's never going to happen.'

Shelley reaches over and takes my hand. She smiles. It means she's with me and understands.

'I'm not even divorced yet,' I say quietly.

'I know. Bad timing aye.'

I nod. I give myself a little shake. 'Tell me why Francesco being part of a rich company means you won't be seeing him again.'

'Oh come on!' There's that *really* look again.

'No, sorry, you're going to have to spell it out for me. He might be rich and handsome, but you're gorgeous. You're also the kindest and most caring person I know. He'd be lucky to have you.'

'The divide is too big. I'm an accounts manager, he's a yacht owner. I shop in Aldi, he flies food in from all over the world just to treat his family. We're worlds apart, Selene.' She gives a big sigh and rests her chin in her hands, elbows on the table.

'Did he ask for your phone number?'

'He did, but he will have only been polite. He won't ring.'

'You never know?'

'Guess not. But anyway, stop taking the fun out of my weekend. No matter what happens I had the best time, I don't regret anything. Now tell me about the rest of your night.'

I groan. 'It didn't go so well in the end.'

'Why not?'

'I thought he was about to tell me that he loved me, so I cut him off. He didn't take it very well.'

'Arr, poor guy. I think it's obvious to everyone that he's in love with you.'

'Poor guy? What about poor me? I made it clear from the beginning I'm not ready for a relationship. Why should I be made to feel bad if he didn't listen?'

'I'm not trying to make you feel bad.'

'Oh I know, sorry, I didn't mean you. He made me feel bad last night when I made it clear at the end of this summer holiday I'm leaving for good.'

'Have you decided what you're going to do when you leave here? You can come back to mine if you like, if you're not ready to get your own place.'

'Thanks, that's lovely of you but I think I am going to get my own place.'

'Do you want me to start house hunting for you?'

Is half a truth a lie? 'No, it's OK, I've already got somewhere in mind.'

'Ooo, exciting me, tell me.'

'Not yet, I kind of want to get things finalized before I tell anyone.'

'Mysterious, love it!'

Two hours later I wave Shelley off as she heads back to Manchester. I've never kept secrets from her before, but I have a feeling that at the moment I should keep things close to my chest.

These are my plans and I'm not going to give anyone the opportunity to talk me out of doing what I want to do.

Last night's brush with a love declaration has galvanized me into forging ahead with my plans. A tinge of mania mingles with my decisions, an almost desperate edge gilds everything I'm about to do.

I open my laptop. Yesterday I received an email. I can't believe how quickly they responded. I couldn't answer it yesterday. Yesterday I was wavering on the edge of indecision, not today. My fingers fly over the keyboard as I type my response. I read it through six times before I press send.

I sit back and stare at the screen. I've made a decision that hasn't been influenced by anyone.

A thought jolts me and I sit up straight. Was that a true statement, or had Giovanni falling in love pushed me into making that decision? I put my hands on my head in sudden alarm. Is this me really making plans for my own future or am I running away?

I stand up and start pacing the room. When nothing but panic fills my head, I decide to go for a run through the forest. I change with lightning speed, check the time and set off.

As soon as I hit the forest path, stress begins to fall away. I try not to think, and instead just soak in the views and scents of the lush green trees. I wonder if people in Cockington realize how lucky they are to have this on their doorstep.

I glance at my watch. Half an hour has gone and I haven't begun to slow yet. I try slowing down, worried I'll get cramp. After two minutes, I speed up again. My trainers are pounding the soft mud path. My arms are pumping by my sides. I am running for my life.

Eventually, that fearful stitch begins to manifest. I slow to a jog, too late, my side is in agony. I stop and rest my hands on my knees. I run all the time, I should know better how to pace myself.

When I finally get my breath back, I straighten up. A breeze is stirring the leaves, it's a thrilling sound. I hear the sound of water and go looking for it. A brook babbles away between rocks and trees. It's the kind of place you hope to find fairies and pixies, with toadstools dotted around in between tall lush green ferns.

How stress-free is the path of nature... it soothes my anxious soul.

As I walk, I begin to analyze my decision and I come to the conclusion that this is what I want to do. Giovanni's declaration might have pushed me to go for it a little earlier than I planned, but still fundamentally this is what I want. Calm descends.

Time to go back, I need to shower before I call Gio.

'Hi.' His voice is a bit standoffish.

'Do you fancy a walk on the beach?'

There's a significant pause before he answers, and I know he had to think about whether he wanted to or not. 'OK, do you know where you would like to go?'

'Not really. Just somewhere close with a long view of the beach and ocean.'

'Are you ready now?'

'Yes.'

'Walk around then, I have the Nissan here.'

'OK, see you in two ticks.'

'I thought we could go to Meadfoot Beach again,' he says as I approach the car.

'Sounds good to me.'

Luckily the drive there doesn't take long because we sit in silence. I can feel his hurt-anger wafting off him, but I don't want to say anything until we're there.

We park up and head straight to the water line. For the first time since I've known him, he doesn't take my hand.

I feel the loss of it and it makes me sad.

We must have been walking along the shore for about fifteen minutes in silence, when Gio finally says, 'You have something you want to talk about?'

OK, deep breath.

'I really like you Gio, and I mean a lot and not just as friends, it's definitely more than that, as I think you know.'

He stays quiet.

'But…' why does bad news always start with but? 'I'm not ready for a new relationship, and I have to be honest with you and tell you I don't know if I ever will be. I want to do something new with my life, and I don't want to be tied down again. I have loved getting to know you, and my God Gio, I have loved how you have opened my eyes to what a relationship can be like. If I had been divorced for years, or maybe if I was still single, I think I would be saying something completely different right now. I don't want to hurt you, I'm really sorry if I have, but I need to leave at the end of my holiday and go in search of me.'

We carry on walking, he doesn't say anything. Sadness is crushing me. I don't want to hurt him. I also don't want to say goodbye just yet, but I'll have to if he can't accept that this is just a holiday romance.

'Are you telling me goodbye?'

I want to hold his hand so bad. 'No I'm not. I'm saying at the end of the holiday I will be leaving.'

'So you're not saying goodbye now, you're saying you will say goodbye at the end of your holiday.'

'Yes.'

'OK.'

'OK?'

'Sure, what did you expect? That I would break down and cry on you?'

'No, I…' Well maybe a little!

'I'm used to holiday flings, Selene. You won't be any different.'

Oh, ouch, that hurt. Fair though, what can I expect?

'Now that we've cleared the air, can we kiss?'

A smile twitches at the corners of my mouth. 'Sure.'

We stop walking and look at each other. His eyes aren't glistening with excitement like normal. They're heavy and dark, I wonder what mine betray. I take a step forward. I'm standing in front of him. He doesn't move just keeps looking at me and I wonder if he's changed his mind.

I reach up and wrap my arms around his neck. I stand on tiptoes when he doesn't lean down. I still can't reach his lips, I need him to move.

Slowly, millimeter by millimeter he moves towards me. Our lips touch, we don't kiss. I'm frightened he is going to pull away, I lean into his body. The touch becomes more. Gently we offer our lips to each other, a surrender to the longings between us.

I know if my life had been different I'd be ecstatic right now. Giovanni has over the last two weeks somehow managed to reach in past all my armored layers and kidnapped my heart and soul. I feel like I belong to him.

But my life has made me who I am. Who I want to be going forward depends on each decision I make today and evermore. I know that if I surrender to Gio fully, I will spend the rest of my life regretting that I didn't find out who I am first. Who knows what life has planned for us? Right now all that matters is that he understands and that he doesn't hate me.

His kiss says he doesn't hate me. I'm grateful.

When we pull away he reaches up and rubs his thumb across my now tender lips. There's a slight smile in his eyes for which I'm very glad.

As we head off up the beach again, I slip my hand into his and he gives it a quick squeeze.

Chapter 30

Giovanni & Selene – A Summer Thing

NOT BEING IN CONTROL creates havoc in my core. It displaces my equilibrium. I'm trying to let Selene take the lead regarding how and when we meet up, but I've got to be honest and admit it's choking me. I like to know where I stand, and with Selene I haven't got a clue. Her body language is positive, not so her words.

I'm struggling with the fact that she doesn't seem to love me.

We haven't seen each other for five days, and I can sense the rift that's grown between us. This was her idea to come to the beach this evening; she made a picnic and got everything ready. I would rather spend the little time I have with her on our own. I want her in my arms. I'm starving for her touch. Some days I don't think I can function.

This close proximity to Selene is bittersweet torture.

I squash sand through my fingers and focus on the grains.

'Do you think Mark has turned you against love?'

I CAN'T TELL GIOVANNI how intoxicating I find him. He's already confused by my mixed signals. Nor do I want to break into an explanation about Mark, the only other person I've had sex with. That's private. But I'm blown away by the difference between them.

I want to tell Gio I love him, but I can't, that just wouldn't be fair. All I can do is express what's inside me without words. My actions will be ambiguous, hard for him to decipher. Yet I hope his spirit will feel mine as I reach out to love him the only way I can right now.

'I think that he has made me miss out on life, but no, I don't think he's turned me against love. I hope to love again, with every fiber of my body, but I'm not ready to find it yet.'

He blows out a long, slow sigh like he's been holding his breath.

'Come and swim with me.' I stand up and offer him my hand. He takes it and I pull him up. 'Come on, let's run in!' I let go of his hand and charge into the sea. Despite the warm day, the water is cold and it snatches my breath. Before I can think of going in slowly, Gio has grabbed me and is pulling me under the waves.

'You!' I yell, as we come up for air. He starts swimming away so I can't return the duck and push him under. I'm straight after him.

He doesn't go too far before he stops and waits for me. I swim up to him.

'You can still stand here,' he says.

I push my feet down but I can only stand on my tiptoes.

'Here,' he says, and pulls me to him.

I wrap my legs around his waist.

I wish there was no space at all between us. The parts of our flesh that touch are tingling. It reminds me of when I went to Malta on holiday and swam in the sea at night. Sparks of light, caused by the phosphorus in the water, sprinkle everywhere when you splash. There's no phosphorus here, but there sure are sparks. It's not a sexual tension though, it's something deeper. A longing to give myself to Gio pumps through my veins. Excitement and sadness spin and churn my insides rising to my chest.

Gio secures me against him. My anchor from the sea's current. Our lips come together, perfect fit, meant for each other. One hand stays firmly on my bum, while the other moves across my back.

I'm glad we're kissing, it stops me thinking. The two halves of me are definitely at war. Miss. Independence wants out of the English Riviera and as far away from Gio as I can get. Miss. Tenderhearted wants Gio to hold her and never let go. Better to kiss, and push away the conflict. Right now, all of me wants *this*.

I tighten my legs around his waist. He moans into our kiss as my hands wrap tightly around his neck. His hand, that has been stroking my back under the water, is slipping downwards. His fingers pull back my bikini bottoms and then slip into the space between my legs. Now it is my turn to moan.

I try to pull back. I hadn't seen anyone on the beach when we came into the water, but I want to double check no one has arrived. His teeth bite my lip, preventing me from pulling back. I relent and return to the kiss.

His fingers push deep inside me. The shock causes me to gasp. I try molding our skin together I'm pushing into him hard. His fingers know exactly what to do until I'm panting and desperately urgent for more inside me than his finger.

We should stop, someone might turn up. I try to pull myself off him again. With an iron grip he holds me firmly in place. I'm flustered, jittery. I want him, but I hadn't planned to do it here. When I look up at him I see he's been waiting for me. Our eyes connect. His pupils are dilated. His lips are shut, he's breathing heavily through his nostrils. Holding my attention, he pulls his fingers again and knocks his swimming shorts down. The hardness of him is against me. I suck in my breath while biting my lip and trying to be quiet. I can't believe we're about to do this. My heart is racing. His hand moves again, guiding himself and then…

Slowly, oh so very slowly, he's pushing himself inside me.

I'm about to turn my head and check no one is watching.

'Don't.' His word is both authoritative and pleading.

I don't turn. I moan. I chew my lip.

He's thrusting fast now, keeping me against him with his strong arms. I'm putty in his hands. I want this. In and out. In and out. Unbelievable sensations flood me as cold water envelopes everything we do and seeps into my normally warm place. In and out.

Oh god I want this.

In and out. My walls start to pull backwards, like the ebbing tide. Back and back, oh god! Gio moans.

'Gio…' I whimper.

We shudder together, releasing our juices at the same time. Too late it dawns on me that we haven't used protection. I don't care. I drop my head against his chest. His hand sneaks up to my hairline and he holds me against him. If I'm pregnant then it's meant to be. I'll change my plans and stay and build a life with Gio… *if* I'm pregnant.

'I love you,' he whispers into my wet hair.

Silent tears mingle with seawater.

When our breathing has returned to normal, he pulls me into his arms and carries me out of the sea. Being carried by Gio is the best feeling in the world. It is home, it's where I belong. It's so confusing.

I'm more than a little relieved when I see we still have the beach to ourselves.

Gently he puts me down. Before I can move he picks up a beach towel and wraps it around me.

He kisses the tip of my nose. 'I hope you've brought lots of food.'

I grin. 'Tons!'

Chapter 31

Selene – Identity

THE GOLD BAND REPRESENTS WIFEHOOD. That very word then defines you as a person. You are no longer just you, you are attached to another, you even take their name. Your identity is linked firmly in the man you now call husband.

Removing the symbol of marriage, to me, seems like ripping off a bandage from a weeping wound. It's raw and hurtful. By taking it off I'm convinced I am losing a part of myself, my identity at least. I know it's wrong but I feel less of a person, empty even. At the beginning of this holiday I couldn't do it.

Today the ring is off. I drop it into my jewelry bag.

I look in the mirror.

I am a blank canvas – that's not a bad thing. It means I can paint and color the new me anyway I want. It's an adventure that I'm looking forward to. I don't need to be a wife to know who I am. I just need courage and determination to allow the real me to grow.

DURING THE LAST FOUR WEEKS I've only seen Gio at the weekends, and then not all the time. It has become much more casual now that he's returned to London. He's been coming down on Thursday nights and we've enjoyed parts of the weekends together. He rarely sleeps over anymore; he's probably only slept at the cottage three times since the fallout, and on those occasions it has been because he's had too much to drink.

His drinking level has risen. I try not to read too much into it. He tells me he doesn't drink in London and just likes to unwind over the weekend. I'm not sure I believe him. There are slight grey smudges under his eyes that never used to be there, and I don't think he's sleeping well.

He tells me everything is fine, every time I ask.

I am relieved that my period came the week after our connection in the sea. For a few days after, all I could think about were babies and weddings. When my time of month turned up I was surprised to find that I was both relieved and disappointed. Women aye!

We've lost part of our connection, Gio and I. It's left a gaping hole in me. Sex is still great and we both enjoy it, well at least I think we both do, I do. But the headiness of it has gone. I find myself daydreaming of the old Gio rather a lot. It sometimes makes being with the new Gio a bit hard.

So hard in fact, that I've decided to cut my holiday short and therein cut the relationship off.

I'm going to tell him at the end of this coming weekend. Just one last bit of our holiday romance and I'll be gone, forever.

On Thursday morning Gio calls me.

'Morning Babe.' He never calls me Bella anymore.

'Hi, how you doing?' He doesn't normally call in the mornings so I automatically imagine something is wrong. I'm right.

'Important clients have requested a meeting today, so I'm not able to drive down.'

My heart drops. I wanted one last weekend together before I left. 'I'm sorry to hear that. Are you going to drive down tomorrow?'

'I can't, I'm meeting them again tomorrow morning. If it runs over I will probably take them out for a meal in the evening.'

'Oh.' All my disappointment fills that word.

Gio misunderstands it. 'Will you miss me?'

'Yes.'

'Good, what I'm thinking is you could jump on a train and be here in no time. I'll get Kevin to pick you up from the station and take you back to the apartment and show you around so you can make yourself at home. We can get a takeaway tonight and stay in. Tomorrow I thought you might like to go shopping or sightseeing and again Kevin will show you around. And then we can meet up for dinner.'

'But you might have to have dinner with your clients.'

'Maybe, but if I do I would like you to be there.'

'Oh I don't know. I'm not really a high-society gal.'

Gio really chuckles. 'No you're not, and that's what I love about you. Please say yes, I want to show off my home to you just once before you disappear.' Sadness tinged the last part of his sentence.

'OK then, why not!'

'Great, can you make your own way here?'

'Of course I can.'

We discuss where Kevin will pick me up and say our goodbyes.

I turn the phone off and stare out of the window for a moment. This is actually perfect. It means he won't be anywhere near here when I leave on Monday morning. Not that he would chase after me once he'd found out I've left early, but the thought of him chasing after me is bittersweet, and I think I would be disappointed if he didn't. Oh contraire!

Chapter 32

Giovanni – Some things you can't Control

KEVIN HAS GONE to pick Selene up. I'm trying my hardest not to think about her, but it's difficult. She has consumed my thoughts since the first time she smiled at me.

The meeting with my American clients goes smoothly. They buy into all my suggestions. We're forming a merger that will be beneficial for both our companies. Not with my parent's company, I never touch the structure of that. It's with one of my own companies. I purchased the haulage company on a whim seven years ago, not really sure what to do with it. Providence was with me when I was introduced to someone who could manage it for me at a networking evening. Roger has been the backbone of that company ever since and I don't know what I would have done without him. This new merger will also restructure his position in the company from managing director to major shareholder, it's only fair. Needless to say he's over the moon and very grateful.

This shift in the company will also free up a lot of my time. Time I'd planned to spend with Selene, time I'll now have to fill with something else. As yet I don't know what that will be.

I've been counting down the days until she leaves. It's a depressing pastime, not one I recommend. A part of me wants to beg her not to go, a larger part of me has too much pride.

Kevin's just messaged to say they're at the flat now. I wonder what she'll think of it, and whether there's any chance she'll like it enough to stay.

Three hours later, I'm in the lift in my apartment block heading up to my bachelor pad. I'm shaking. God damn nerves! I shake out my hands to try and knock the stupid nervousness out of them.

I hold my hands out in front of me. They're steady. Not so my heart that is racing. The lift door opens and I enter the apartment. I'm struck by the aromas of cooking. I walk through the hallway towards the kitchen where I can hear Selene singing along to Bon Jovi. I smile, that woman has an eclectic taste when it comes to music.

She's at a counter which means she has her back to me.

I love that she's at home in my kitchen. Nearly all my ex's have been the type of women who want to be catered for. I don't remember a single one of them ever cooking for me – and I was with Jojo for nearly eighteen months.

She must have heard me because she turns around.

'Hi you,' she says.

'Hey, how's it going?'

'Fine, I thought I'd cook, you don't mind do you?'

'Oh course not, smells amazing. Do you have everything you need?'

She brushes back a stray strand of hair with the back of her hand. 'As a matter of fact, no, I'm dying for a drink, but blow me if I can find any alcohol anywhere.'

I laugh. 'Come with me.'

In the area connecting the kitchen to the dining room is a row of floor-to-ceiling cupboards that are designed to appear like a plain wall. I tap one of them and a door opens. Behind it is a huge wine refrigerator; I tap another one which is full only of Champagne bottles.

'Jesus!'

I grin as I move along opening more that reveal a red wine section and one that opens out like a bar and is full of hard liquor. 'Take your poison.'

'I'm cooking chicken escallops with parmentier potatoes and salad. Either white or rosé whichever you prefer.'

I don't hesitate and pull out a bottle of Château Galoupet Cru Classé, I wonder if she'll remember it.

'Nice choice,' she says standing on her tiptoes to plant a kiss on my cheek. 'I really enjoyed the last bottle we had.'

I'm glad she recognized it. 'You didn't have to cook you know.'

'I like cooking and I'm a bit regretful that I haven't been able to cook for you more, so here I am.'

'Those potatoes smell good.'

'It's the garlic and rosemary, once you've tried my parmentier potatoes you won't want potatoes any other way!'

I can believe that. I know for sure that now I've tasted Selene no other woman will ever do for me.

Since returning to London I've called Coco twice. Each time we had fun clubbing and drinking, even kissing, but when it came time for her to earn her money I paid her and sent her home. I just couldn't do it. I guess Selene has zapped all of *that* guy out of me, and I'm not sure if he's ever coming back.

'How did the meeting go?'

I open the bottle as Selene goes back to preparing a salad. 'Very well, thanks. We closed the deal today so they've changed their plans and they've gone to Scotland for a game of golf. I'm free tomorrow after all.'

'Yeah!' She seems genuinely pleased. In fact, everything about her seems comfortable and relaxed. Has she changed her mind about leaving me? A knot that's been in my spine for the last four weeks comes undone. I sit down at the breakfast bar and watch her cook. She's dipping the chicken breasts in egg, flour, and breadcrumbs. Her cheeks are rosy and she seems happy.

A rush of exuberance hits me, which I instantly squash. I can't hope. If she doesn't stay around it will crush me as it is.

We eat dinner outside on the balcony overlooking the park. London is noisy and grimy and you have to shower every day, but I love it.

'To holidays,' I say lifting my glass.

We clink them together. 'To holidays,' she says quietly and then smiles at me. Her eyes are glistening. I haven't seen that in four weeks, something has definitely changed. I want to ask her outright. I don't like games, not that I think she's playing games she's been too straight with me about her plans for that since the start.

But I'm a man who likes to be in control, and I see my psychiatrist once a month to keep my anxieties at bay. Only my closest family members know this about me, that and my OCD which I battle with every day.

Like now, leaving the balcony door open because Selene's here, is so hard. Normally, I would automatically close it behind me when I came out here, to keep dust from entering.

On the outside I look calm, it's taken years of practice to accomplish. Inside, I'm flapping around like a bird trapped in a cage. The only thing I can master about all this is the fact that I don't let anyone see it; hence I have claimed back a semblance of control.

These are the things I noticed as I walked across my apartment when I first got home. Selene left her shoes by the front door. That she didn't walk over my plush white carpet in her shoes I appreciate, that she left them by the door and didn't put them away makes my skin crawl. She left her handbag on one of the sofas, her bracelets by the kitchen sink, and she's dropped a piece of lettuce on the floor and not noticed because it sits there winking and laughing at me. I couldn't bend down to pick it up in front of her, it would reveal too much. She's also been through the bookcase and three books have been left on the coffee table.

Do I love Catherine? Wholeheartedly. Whether she knows I have problems or just thinks me fussy-beyond-reason I don't know. But she keeps everything shipshape for me and sometimes I don't think I pay her enough.

I lift my wine glass. 'This is the best holiday romance I've ever had.' And that's the truth.

Selene lifts her, and as we clink says, 'This is the only holiday romance I've ever had.'

And that does it. I stand and offer my hand which she takes.

Things in the bedroom have been a bit strange for us in the last four weeks as I've tried to nail down and hide my desperation. Tonight things feel different and that edge is taken off me.

I use the remote control to draw the curtains, dim the lights and put low music on. When I look up she is standing only in her lingerie, matching bra and undies of red satin. She's been sunbathing and her skin's sun-kissed brown. Her stunning red hair flows over her shoulders. My little firecracker looks like a titan goddess!

I undress, stopping to hang my clothes up. She doesn't say anything, she just waits.

When I turn back to her I'm overcome with need and desire. I run my hands through her hair and grip the back of her neck and pull her towards me. We kiss. It's unlike any kiss we've had before. Somehow I can feel her pouring herself into me through this kiss. I chew her lip. She tugs at my tongue. I explore every tiny part of her mouth. She bends towards me. I scoop her up into my arms and carry her to the bed. On the way she unclips her bra and lets it drop to the floor. I'll pick it up later.

Tonight I feel like it's the first time we've been together. She shudders under every kiss and touch, and gasps when I suck her breasts, arching her back and moaning like I've never done it before.

Urgency seems to charge through her. She sits up and pushes me back. I'm willing and lie still as her mouth explores my body. Her beautiful mouth takes me to a place of ecstasy, but I stop her before I explode. I want to bring her to a place of sexual surrender. I will master her... if only for a while.

I explore every tiny aspect of her body. She squeals for release. 'Please,' she begs. I ignore. I am intent on pulling her strings until she can bear it no more. 'Please.'

I kiss inside her thigh as my hands roam her body. She's lifting her hips, thrusting at me, demanding I fill her. I continue kissing her legs. She moans. 'Oh, Gio, please.'

I climb over her. She opens her eyes. Her pupils are dilated, her mouth is slightly open, her chest rising and falling in quick succession. My firecracker wants me, and who am I to deny her?

I slip inside. We both moan.

Every bit of love I feel for her is driven in those thrusts. Can you feel it Selene? Do you feel my love? I thrust, she arches her back. Her eyes stay fixed on mine.

I love you, do you hear me, I love you! Shivers wrack my body as I collapse on top of her.

'My God! Gio, that was something else!'

I can't answer.

I should drop my pride and beg her to stay.

I'm not able to.

Instead, my soul pleads silently – will you stay with me? Please.

Chapter 33

Selene – The Ex

I'VE ONLY BEEN TO LONDON a few times before and only been sightseeing with my parents when I was little. Shelley and I have come a couple of times to take in a show, which I love doing. But we usually just watch a show and grab a meal, there's never anything beyond that.

That's why I get up when Gio does at five, even though he tries to persuade me to stay in bed, I want to go and explore.

'Kevin doesn't start work until eight, and trust me everywhere is closed at this time of day.'

'That's OK, I want to see London before she wakes up. I'm planning on going for a jog in Hyde Park.'

'It's not safe at this time in the morning.'

'Alright, I'll wait a couple of hours.'

His frown says he doesn't believe me. I give him my *sweet* smile, which makes him laugh.

'I should be finished about two-thirty. Tell me what you'd like to do and I'll plan something.'

'I'll have a think and text you later.'

'Will you go back to sleep?'

'I'll try.'

He kisses me on the forehead and I feel like a proper couple, the thought takes a little joy out of me.

When he's gone I explore his apartment. I can't help it. I want to learn all about him. I want to build my picture of him up, so I never forget him. I rifle through his walk-in closet and goes through all his drawers. Everything is immaculate. Clean and stored with precision. It's a good job he can't see my old wardrobes! All my stuff is currently in a storage unit. I wonder if I should just donate it all to charity and start afresh?

I go around all his walls touching for hidden doors. One pops open and it is a walk-in coat cupboard. Who has one of those? When I'm finished nosing around, I make a cafetière of coffee and go and sit on the balcony to watch London wake up.

It's so noisy on the balcony and I realize how great Gio's soundproofing is. Trucks and cars and people talking, and it's only six! I compare it to Cockington and wonder how Gio can live here when he's got access to a little piece of Heaven.

Giovanni's flat is quite impersonal, with a lot of white and chrome, quite masculine. But on one wall several frames display different family photos. I pick a small square frame off the wall. It's a picture of Gio and his brothers and sister. I don't think it can be very old as they still look the same now. I run my finger over Gio's face.

'I'm going to miss you.' Emotions flow and bring on the tears. I wipe them away. 'Please understand, Gio.' I have an idea and fetch my phone. Carefully, I take the picture out of the frame and take several photos of it with my phone. I pick the clearest one and then crop it so that it is just Gio's face. I save them all to my photos and then put the photograph back in the frame and rehang it. Beside the picture by the waterfall, this is the only photo of Gio I will have when I go on my adventure.

I can't wait any longer and decide to go for a jog. I put the postcode in maps on my phone and discover it's only a twenty-minute walk away, so ten minutes if I'm jogging. The route on the phone takes me past the Ritz. Wow, I didn't realize yesterday that Gio lived right in the heart of it all.

I run alongside Green Park and then cross the road into Hyde Park. It's already fairly busy with lots of runners and a few cyclists. I love exploring and discovering somewhere new. I set a steady pace and make my way through a place that carries history in its every blade of grass. I imagine the Victorian times and the rich parading along the very path I'm jogging on.

When I've had enough I grab a coffee and find a quiet bench overlooking the Serpentine. Ducks swim around me, probably hoping I've got bread. Birds are tweeting and it's hard to remember I'm in the center of the city.

I people watch, wondering where they're all going. Whether they're happy or stressed, are they content with their lot in life?

I feel peaceful.

I've made my plans for my future.

All that remains is this last twenty-four hours with Gio because I have to go back to the cottage tomorrow. I head back to the flat and take a much-needed shower.

I send Gio a text. I know what I want to do: *Can we be tourists? I'd really like to go to Madam Tussauds and take a ride on the London Eye xx*

I can imagine him groaning.

He texts back: *Sure, see you soon xx*

Oh he's good to me!

Madam Tussauds' is super cheesy, but also great fun. We mess about and laugh our way around it, stopping to take photos posing with the stars and the famous, using all the props left for staging photographs.

I want to get the underground to the London Eye, he puts his foot down. I laugh and give in, and we jump into a black cab.

'It says in the tour guide that the underground is the only way to travel.'

'I don't care what it says, it's a taxi or I call Kevin to drive us.'

I laugh at him and put my arm through his, and then I turn my attention to the window to soak in all the sights.

We have to queue to go on the Eye and I can sense Gio getting fidgety. 'Have you been on before?'

'No.'

We eventually get on. It moves so slow I want to get out and push it. We're also in a cabin with about ten other people. It feels crowded and I'm beginning to wish we'd done something else.

He peeks at me out of the corner of his eye and I can see he's amused. 'Not what you thought?'

I shake my head. 'Not at all.'

He wraps his arm around my shoulder and just like that it doesn't matter where we are or what we're doing. All that matters is we're together, enjoying the moment.

'I think I prefer the English Riviera,' I say as we walk away.

'Me too.'

'That surprises me. If that's true why don't you move there permanently?'

'It's complicated.'

'Really? Like I'm stupid and I wouldn't understand?'

'Don't be so defensive. I'm a private man. I don't broadcast my thoughts and reasons. London suits me right now. I don't need to justify that to anyone.'

Maybe it's providence we're not getting together. 'I could never live in London.'

'I work here.'

'Yes, but you could work from anywhere if you put your mind to it.'

'You don't know what I want. I'm perfectly happy.'

'Are you though? Because you've not been coming across as happy these last few weeks.'

'And whose fault is that?' He glares at me.

Damn, I walked into that one.

'Does work make you happy then?'

He thinks about it for a little while as we continue walking alongside the Thames.

'It used to,' he finally says, and I feel sad for him.

'Maybe it's time to find some new sort of work that will make you happy again?'

'Umm.' Uncommitted, and I wonder what he's thinking. 'Are you going to tell me what you're going to do next? Or are you keeping it a secret?'

Definitely a secret. 'I'm not a hundred percent sure yet, but I'm thinking of applying for a job overseas.'

He pulls us to a stop and stares down at me. 'Where are you going?'

'I don't know yet. I haven't even got a job. There's a vacancy in Ireland, but I don't know if they'll offer it to me. Nothing is decided yet.' It's a lie but I just can't bring myself to tell him the truth.

I can see he's unhappy but he doesn't say anything else. We start walking again. He stops and sends a message to someone on his phone. 'Let's wait here.'

'What are we waiting for?'

'Kevin.'

'Oh.'

'You're going back tomorrow, right?'

'Yep.'

'Right then, I would like to take you for a meal tonight at the Connaught.'

'Is that a restaurant?'

'It's a hotel. The restaurant is run by Hélène Darroze, her cooking is something else. I'd like you to try it.'

'Is she a better cook than me?'

He grins at me and then when he sees my face starts laughing. 'Just a touch, but you're a very close second!'

'Good.'

He leans down and gives me a peck on the lips, and everything is put right again… for a little while.

'Do I need fancy clobber?'

'You look stunning in anything.'

'Do I?'

'It's upmarket, but you'll be fine in anything, honest.'

'What are you wearing?'

'I thought maybe Bermuda shorts and a Hawaiian shirt.'

'Pah!'

'A boring old suit.'

'OK.'

'Do you want to go shopping?'

'No thanks. I brought something that might be appropriate.'

'I'm sure it will be.'

I don't know where Kevin has been, but he's suddenly in the street behind us. 'That was quick.'

Gio opens the door for me. 'I like to keep him close.'

An hour later we're ready to go. I'd asked to get ready in one of the guest suites so I didn't feel uncomfortable putting on my makeup. When I walk into the lounge, Gio is standing in front of the patio doors looking out over London. He turns and I see his look of approval. It makes me feel good.

Gio doesn't know how much money I have. We've never talked about it, but truthfully I have enough so that I wouldn't have to work again if I didn't want to. But I do. You see dad won the lottery a year before he died. My parents had never been big spenders, so they purchased a detached house they loved and then invested the rest for my future. I might not have loads of money like the Giacomellis' but I'm very comfortable.

The outfit I've brought along with me reflects just how much money I have. My evening purse alone cost £1,500. I didn't hesitate at the time I purchased it, but the last few weeks have changed me and I know I will never spend that amount of money on a purse again. My money is going towards other things now.

My dress is a silver halter-neck, ruched over the body, and then opening up to a flat flare, with a slit that reaches the top of my right thigh. With ultra-high heels and my hair piled on top of my head, I feel tall and elegant. I've done my makeup to the best of my ability and I think I've got the smoky eyes almost as good as Shelley does them.

Gio's look of approval tells me I've not done so bad. Not that I need his approval, but I'm glad he appreciates the effort. He looks handsome himself in a deep blue, clean-cut suit. Boy, but I love a man in a suit!

He offers me his arm and we leave.

As we stand in the elevator, wafts of sandalwood and cedarwood, combined with bergamot musk flow around me with alluring sweetness. Gio doesn't always wear cologne, and I'm loving this one. Its rugged, fresh scent thrills me. It's rich and heady and right now all I want to do is kiss him. If you could bottle 'hunk' then this is the smell.

A chauffeured car waits to take us to the restaurant. Giovanni, ever the gentleman, opens the door and waits for me to get in, before closing in and coming around the other side.

Not long after we set off, Gio takes something out of his pocket and hands me a small flat box.

'What's this?'

'It's something to remind you of me when you're off on your travels.'

A thrill runs through me. I don't care if it's just this box, he thought of me going away and got me a gift when all I thought he wanted to do was argue with me.

Inside is a plain silver band bracelet, but when I look closely I see that the outer band is engraved with lots of tiny horseshoes.

That's so sweet. I look at Gio, trying not to cry.

'Look on the inside.'

I lift the band and try reading the inside, but my eyes are brimming with water and it's too hard to see.

'Here.' Gio takes the bracelet and slips it on my wrist. 'It says – A summer romance but a lifetime of memories, love Gio.'

'I need a tissue.' I'm trying to undo the clasp of my evening bag.

Gio does it for me and passes me out a handkerchief. I dab at my eyes. I can't cry I'll look like a panda all night.

When my emotions are finally under control I grab his hand and squeeze it tight. 'I'll never forget you, Gio.'

'I should hope not.'

I'm glad when we arrive. Before the maître d' shows us to our table I ask where the restrooms are. I need to make sure my face is on straight before we sit down.

Satisfied everything is in order, I head back to the restaurant. I stop halfway. Giovanni is in a discussion with probably the most stunning woman I have ever seen. She's in a tight-fitting mini dress showing off legs that go on for miles. She's obviously of mixed race, and her skin is perfectly light-tanned, she is knock-out gorgeous and I've no doubt this is someone that Giovanni has been intimate with. She keeps touching his arm, and then her hair, it's like she's weaving an invisible web that declares to everyone they're an item.

Gio suddenly sees me and takes a step back from the woman. She turns to see what he's looking at and frowns when she clocks me staring at them.

All sorts of crazy stuff is going on inside me right now. I can't believe how jealous I'm feeling. Which is stupid because I'm leaving and of course his life is going to carry on as before, why wouldn't it?

I straighten up and walk towards them with swagger, girl you may be every man's dream, but right now I'm *this* man's dream!

When I reach them, I hook my arm through Gio's. The woman puts her hands on skinny-ass hips.

Oh, she's not happy!

'I thought you said you weren't dating for a while?' she barks.

'I'm not,' answers Gio with a shrug.

Now ain't that the truth!

'Well, what's this then?' She wags her finger at each of us, I wonder if she knows her glare makes her damn right ugly.

'We're just friends about to have dinner,' answers Gio. 'Now if you will excuse us, I believe Bernard is waiting to show us to our table.'

She puts a hand on Gio's chest to stop him from walking away. 'If you're just friends then you won't mind if I give you a kiss goodnight.'

Before either of us can react, she nudges me off Gio's arm and takes his face in her hands and starts to kiss him, rather passionately.

Heat is rising from my chest to my cheeks. He could push her away!

Eventually, he does, but bright lipstick is all over his mouth.

'Oh, baby,' she says, 'let me get that for you.' She uses her thumb to wipe it off his lips. 'Be seeing you soon, lover.'

With that last remark she strolls away. I might have tried swagger when I was approaching them, but she oozes sensuality with every sway of her hips.

'Who walks like that!' I blurt out, not expecting an answer.

Gio laughs. 'Models do.'

That makes sense; only models would be that skinny.

'Shall we?' Gio asks. I can't believe he's smiling. I want to hit his stupid face right now.

Chapter 34

Giovanni – Green Eyes

I CAN'T BELIEVE JOJO KISSED ME! But Selene's green eyes are sparkling right now with anger. I know she's cross at me for kissing someone else, but the fact that she's jealous is doing my damaged ego some good.

'Are you going to tell me who that was?'

Oh my feisty firecracker, how I love it when you're worked up. I can't keep the grin off my face. She kicks me under the table.

'Oww,' I laugh, 'what was that for?'

She shrugs. 'I don't know. Just stop laughing already!'

'OK, I'll try, just hang on a moment.' Bernard is hovering with the wine menu. 'Bernard we'll just have a bottle of Cristal please.'

He nods and leaves.

'That was Jojo.'

'Oh, the eighteen-month one.'

'Yep, that's her.'

The wind is going out of Selene's sails. I don't want that. I want her to stay jealous. 'She thinks we'll end up together eventually.'

'And what do you think?'

'I think we never know what's just around the corner.'

'That's not an answer.'

'It's the only one I'm giving. Are you jealous?'

She folds and unfolds her napkin, trying to work out how to respond.

'Would you be jealous if some man kissed me in front of you?'

'So jealous I would probably kill him.'

Her lips twitch as she tries not to smile. But I know her well now, and I know that answer pleased her.

Dinner, as expected, is wonderful. Selene delights in all the delicate flavors and I delight in her.

On the way back to the apartment we hold hands and don't talk. I think maybe we have both said all we can to each other.

'Would you like an Amaro?'

'Yes please.'

I grin as I pour two nifty measures into glasses. I think that our Italian ways are rubbing off on her. I pass her a glass. 'Saluti.'

'Saluti,' she replies as we clink our drinks. 'I will admit that this bitter-sweet flavor is growing on me, although I still prefer Tia Maria as an after-dinner drink.'

'Would you like to sit on the balcony?'

'Not really, it's too noisy out there, do you mind?'

'Of course not.'

I hang up my jacket and put away my tie and come back in to find Selene reclining on the sofa.

'Space for two?'

She smiles and moves over. 'Always,' she says.

I put my arm out and she moves to my side. We sit in comfortable silence for a while, watching the flames on the fire image flickering in front of us where a fireplace might have been. You could believe it was a real fire, it's just a screen though.

'Thank you for a lovely time.'

I kiss the top of her head. 'You're welcome, and thank you for coming up. I'm glad you got to see my place.' I wish you were staying. 'How long have we got left?' I know that she's paid for the cottage for another six weeks, but something in me wants to check.

She stiffens slightly in my arms and then relaxes again. 'A while yet.'

'Shall we go to bed?'

She nods.

I stand and offer her my hand, and we go into the comfort of my bedroom.

After washing in the bathroom and cleaning our teeth, we slip naked beneath the crisp sheets.

Selene lies on her back, and I lean on my elbow and look down at her. I'm running out of time to get her to surrender to love. I wish I could find the key to unlock the door to Selene's heart. I've got so much anger towards

Mark, it's hard to contain. I bludgeon the punching bag to bits in the gym imagining that it's him.

I'm the first to admit I have issues with women in general and haven't treated them very well in the past. I've kept them at arm's length, putting them all in the same box. I never thought I would love someone like this. Selene has come as a surprise, but where love should bring happiness I am going through mountains of frustrated pain. This pain is the very reason why I have remained a bachelor till now. How am I going to cope when she goes?

All I have is right now, this moment. I need to hold onto it and ensure the memory will last me a lifetime. I nuzzle into her neck and trail a row of kisses along it.

Our dance of love begins. I kiss all her arousal trigger spots until she's moaning and squirming in delight. After a while, Selene pushes me away and we change positions. Her red-hot lips move across my chest and down my abs. The pleasure she gives me nearly blows my mind.

It's hard to remember how shy she was the first time we made love. Afraid to open up and let herself feel. Scared to let me see her naked. That's all gone now. My little firecracker's rotating hips bursts all sorts of erotic desires within me. This part of herself she gives me freely.

But where lies her heart? Why will she not peel back the wall and let me in? I would treat it so carefully, this precious part of her. I would not trample on her esteem as others have done. Nor would I damage her fragile soul. I would do all the things I could to restore her self-confidence and to watch her blossom. Oh to do that... I would gladly pale. I know now what it is to love a woman, to love beyond expression, to long for her with every fiber of my body.

We switch rolls again. I need to master her body even if I fail to master her heart. My teeth nip her skin, she gasps. The link between pain and pleasure brought very thin.

The animal in me rises. I kiss, bite, suck, and work my fingers inside her until her groans are loud and out of control.

By the time I have brought her to climax, she's crying. Tears stream down her cheeks. I try to kiss them away. I don't ask what causes them. It is enough that I have stirred her soul.

For a long time afterward, we lie entangled around each other, legs and arms clamping our bodies as close together as we can get them.

She is the other half of my soul.

Where she goes I will have to follow, though she may not want me to.

She is the breath that fills my lungs.

I cannot imagine life without her.

When it's obvious that neither of us want to go to sleep I ask her, 'Would you like something to drink?'

'Water would be wonderful.'

I thought she would stay in bed, but she rises with me and wraps a bathrobe around her. I pull on a clean pair of boxers and we go to the kitchen together.

In the hours that most people sleep, we sit there and talk about anything and everything. I try my hardest to implant her face into my memory. We laugh, we get quiet, and all the time I think we're saying goodbye although I know that's not right, we have weeks left yet.

'Do you want to borrow any of my books?' Three of them still remain on the coffee table.

'Maybe one day, but not now. I can't believe you have an original copy of Pride and Prejudice; it must have cost you a fortune. Did you read it?'

'I did.'

'And did you enjoy it?'

'Mostly, it was a bit sugary for me. I much prefer Dickens.'

'I didn't find any poetry on your shelves.'

'No it's not really me.'

'None of it?' Selene gives me a skeptical smirk and recites:

> *'I haven't really found any that captures my imagination.'*
>
> *'A sudden blow: the great wings beating still*
>
> *Above the staggering girl, her thighs caressed*
>
> *By the dark webs, her nape caught in his bill,*
>
> *He holds her helpless breast upon his breast.*
>
> *How can those terrified vague fingers push*
>
> *The feathered glory from her loosening thighs?*
>
> *And how can body, laid in that white rush,*
>
> *But feel the strange heart beating where it lies?'*

'Who is that?'

'It's *Leda and the Swan* by *William Yeats (1923).*'

'And you learnt it off by heart?'

'I love the Irish poets. Some works speak to my soul and really move me.'

'I think I'll have to start reading some.'

She taps the end of my nose with her finger. 'You should.'

We go on to discuss all the books we've either loved or hated and why. Vast swathes of understanding flow from our revelations.

When light begins to spill through the patio doors and we know we have talked the night away, she asks me to put *Leonard Cohen* on.

My place is huge. We have loads of space to waltz to *Dance me to the end of love.* I move us across the floor, but not very much. We are more swaying in each other's arms. Her head rests on my shoulder. I feel her tears trickle down my chest. I put my hand on the back of her head and wish for the thousandth time that I could take all her pain away.

'I love you,' I whisper into her hair.

She doesn't answer.

Chapter 35

Selene – Unexpected

I DON'T KNOW HOW I managed to leave Giovanni without breaking down. I think only the knowledge that I was heading towards something new enabled me to go. I fought with the longing to tell him I was going and to let him know where to. In the end I decided this was better. A clean cut. He'd soon get over me and who knows he might even get back together with Jojo, she plainly still wants him.

The train forces me to sit still and ponder my choices. *My* choices, how fab that sounds. If you didn't know what kind of cage I'd stepped out from under you might think me crazy. But a lifetime of saying yes and no in the wrong places has built like a volcano, now my life is flowing through my head and escaping. Showing me that I *can* be whoever I want to be.

When I get back to the cottage I'll tell Shelley all my plans, I'm sure she'll be excited for me. I'm going on a charity mission to help build schools in Kenya. I've had my jabs and got my malaria tablets. Unbeknown to anyone else I've purchased everything I need, which now fills a massive rucksack in the trunk of my car. I'm going to Kenya – argh! How crazy is that? I've applied for positions in several charitable companies and two I've already had Zoom interviews with. They both went well. They know

I'm off to Kenya for three months now and that doesn't seem to be a problem.

As well as paying for myself to go on this trip, I joined a scheme to help pay for someone else who wants to go but can't afford it. The fees, besides the flights and food, all go to the villages to help with the projects, so I was happy to sponsor someone. Elsie will be meeting up with me at Heathrow Airport in two days' time! I can't believe it. I can't believe I'm flying to Africa on my own. Well with Elsie, but mostly I feel like I will be on my own.

'WHAT DO YOU MEAN you're pregnant?' Oh Lord, this is terrible. 'Right I'm coming. I'll be with you tonight.'

'Selene, slow down and let me speak.'

'Are you keeping it?' Lots of mixed feelings about that question.

'Selene!'

'Sorry, sorry, you talk, I'll listen.'

'I don't want you to come back… before you get all hurt, hear me out. My parents know and they've been wonderful. Mum is coming with me to all my appointments. Dad built a crib for me last week.'

'Last week? Last week?'

'I know, I know. You've got your own shit going on right now Selene, and I didn't want to confuse you or get in the way of your plans.'

'You don't even know what I'm planning.'

'No, but I do know you well enough to know you're leaving and you're not telling me where to.'

How on earth can she read me so well? 'I think there's a possibility that Gio may come looking for me when I'm gone. I just thought if you don't know where I am then he wouldn't be able to squeeze the information out of you. Not that you would tell him of course, but I just thought it would be easier if you didn't have to lie.'

'No worries, I get it.'

'But obviously I'm not going now. I'm coming back to help you.'

'No you're not. I don't mean to be rude but I can manage without you. In fact I've enough on my plate without worrying about you. Just come home when you're ready. Buy a house near me and we'll go from there. You're going to be a godmother, so you'll have to come home for the christening.'

'Yikes, this is real? You're going to be a mum!'

'I am. And you know what, I'm excited, how about that? I didn't even know I wanted kids but the moment I found out I was pregnant I've been on a high.'

'Arr, that's so wonderful, Shelley. I'm pleased for you.'

'Thanks.'

'Shelley, can I ask? Who is the father?'

'Can't you guess?'

'Not Francesco!'

'Yes it is. I haven't been with anyone else in the last six months.'

'But you were only here a month ago, is that enough time to get a positive result.'

'Yep, eight days after your period's due gives you an accurate reading.'

'OMG Shelley, this is huge. What are you going to do?'

'I'm not going to tell him, and you have to swear to me that you won't tell anyone. Promise me, right now.'

'OK, I promise.'

'I mean it Selene. I don't want Francesco to think I trapped him or anything. My parents are happy to help me out. I'm going to do this on my own.'

'I want to help.'

'Sweetie, I love you very much, but your head is not screwed on right now. Whatever it is you're planning on doing I want you to go ahead and do it. I will be here when you get back.'

'I feel like I'm deserting you in your hour of need.'

Shelley laughs. 'You're not. I have a large family as you know, so I'm surrounded by people who love me and will love little Cleo when she comes along.'

'Cleo? You know it's a girl already?'

She chuckles. 'I don't know for sure but I just feel it in my waters.'

'Why Cleo?'

Shelley sighs. 'It's the name of Francesco's favorite aunty. He said if he ever had a girl he wanted to call her Cleo.'

'You've got to tell him.'

'NO! And you mustn't either. If he liked me he would have at least sent me a text by now. I've not heard a word from him and I'm certainly not chasing.'

'You don't think he should know?'

'What he doesn't know won't hurt him.'

'Oh Shelley, it doesn't feel right. Are you sure about all this?'

'I'm thirty-six and I've just about given up on ever finding my Mr. Right, which means my dreams for a family were fading fast. I can't begin to explain the joy I feel at being pregnant, Selene. I'm literally brimming over with tears of joy every day. My mum is a nervous wreck, LOL.'

'So long as you're sure.'

'I am.'

'I'll come and see you when the baby is born.'

'Not before?'

'I will if I can, but I'm not a hundred percent sure where I'm going to be.'

'Just ring me from time to time will you, and let me know you're OK?'

'I will.'

'I love you girlfriend.'

'I love you too.'

Chapter 36

Selene – Tough Choices

ALL MY LIFE I have given in to the will of others, mainly my mum and Mark, but also employers and some friends. Throughout this summer break I have been analyzing myself. I can't work out where the need to please people originated, nor why I have found it impossible to say no when someone asked me to do something.

My life is the sum of all my decisions, and of all the times I have said yes in the wrong moments. All the times I gave in, and didn't voice my wants or needs.

Mum, bless her, has dominated a lot of my memories. I think I get her now, thanks to Maria, but I wish I'd had more understanding when she was alive. I want to say sorry for all the times I rejected her, but it's too late and that fills me with sadness.

Mark stole years from me, I still feel that ache, but I've looked back and now I can see all the times that I just let it all happen. Where was my backbone? My pride? My common-sense?

Plus I've been looking backward for a few weeks now with a clear head. I can see the good times too. All the little things Mark did to make me happy, from flowers to holidays to massaging my feet. I thought back then they were expressions of his love. I realize now they were expressions of his guilt. But whatever the stem cause, Mark did a pile of things to make me happy. My hate-level towards him has sunk by at least seventy degrees.

What have I learned these past weeks? I've learned to like myself! I'm not a bad person, maybe a bit weak sometimes, but that's going to change. I've learned I'm never going to be Constable or Picasso, but that doesn't matter either because I've discovered a new hobby that I love.

In fact the list of things I like to do has soared because of Giovanni, I owe him so much. Canoeing was the biggest surprise to me, never thought I would love it so much.

I don't feel ugly anymore. I recognize that actually, some men do find me attractive, and that has soared my confidence to go into the world on my own.

And that… is what I have decided I need.

I want to explore the world and grow as a person. I want to study both in books and in life. I want more than the humdrum of being a stay-at-home wife, nothing wrong with that if that is what brings you joy. But it didn't bring me joy, maybe because I never had children, but probably because I was with a man who didn't really love me and that has tainted my view of love and marriage, who knows? All I know is that I want more… and I'm going to go in search of it.

I CAN'T BRING MYSELF to leave without saying goodbye to Maria. I don't know why, but something urges me to hand back my key in person and say goodbye.

The door is opened by Teresa.

'Is Maria in?'

She nods. 'Go on in, she's expecting you.'

'She is?'

Teresa just smiles and shuts the door.

Maria is sitting on the veranda on a wicker chair with a tall heart-shaped back. I go through the patio doors.

She glances at my hand that is clutching the key to the cottage, and then back up at my face. 'You're leaving us.' It's not a question.

I gulp. 'Yes, it's time for me to go.'

'You will break his heart you know.'

'I didn't mean to. I never set out thinking he would fall in love with me.'

'And yet he has.'

I don't know what to say, this isn't my fault, it isn't.

'Vieni qui.' She points to the chair next to hers.

I sit and then offer her the key, which she lifts her chin to tell me to put it on the table, which I do.

'We were hoping your friend would visit again before you left.'

'Shelley?'

'Sì.'

'Who is *we*?'

'Francesco and me.'

'He hasn't contacted her.' I can't help the bitterness that comes out. I know they don't know about Shelley's condition but I'd like to hit him over the head with the news.

'He's a spoiled child. He hasn't learned yet that the things worth having are the things you need to fight for.'

The secret sits in my chest like a hot coal lump, but I promised and I don't say anything.

'Give me your hand child.'

I offer her my right hand. She lifts it up and places my palm against her cheek. I feel her love pouring through her pores. My chest begins to rise and fall as different emotions jostle for first place within me.

She takes my hand and holds it in both of hers, and then places it against her chest.

Her lined face holds eyes that seem eternally young yet aged with wisdom. 'If you don't find'a your 'appiness, then you must return. Giovanni will'a wait for you, this I know as sure as I need air to breathe. We are'a your famiglia now, Selene. We are'a your home. Come back to us when you are'a ready.'

I can't speak. My chin is wobbling and tears pour from the corners of my eyes. The lump in my throat tells me that if I open my mouth I will not be able to talk.

I stand up, and then lean over to kiss her three times on each cheek. My tears wet her face.

'Addio per ora.'

I nod. It's all I can do. And then I'm running out of the house. I race as if the Devil is after me, for if I stay just one more moment I will never be able to leave… and I will hate myself forever.

Giovanni – Everything Changes

'BREATHE, GIO, BREATHE.'

I'm trying, I'm gulping but I can't feel anything in my lungs. I'm empty. I bend over and drop my hands onto my knees.

'Mio figlio vieni qui.'

Slowly, I straighten and approach the bed.

'Sedersi.'

I do as I'm bid and sit on the edge of Nonna's bed.

'Gio, what'a do they say about birds in cages?'

'That they don't sing.'

'And what'a do they say about letting people go?'

'If it was meant to be they'll come back to you. But she's the other half of my soul, Nonna. I'm no longer complete without her.'

Nonna reaches for my hand. I stare at the veins and age spots as she strokes my arm and hand. I feel her pouring love into me. It's a soothing tonic.

'Selene isn't ready for commitment, amore mio. She has'a just left one cage; she's not'a ready for another.'

'I wouldn't put her in a cage, Nonna. I would put her on a pedestal.'

'Oh, how'a the eyes of youth do not see. For a clever man, you are'a sometimes a stupido boy.'

'Nonna!' I'm slightly hurt.

'She's on a journey to find her equal.'

'I could be that man!'

'You could, and you very well may be. But love is about more than two people meeting. It is about timing, and about being ready at the same time.'

'I love her, Nonna.'

When my grandfather died I cried in the privacy of my London apartment, the last time I cried in public was when I was six and I fell off my bike. Lorenzo had laughed at me that day, and called me a cry-baby. It was the last time anyone has seen a tear fall from my eyes.

Now, I'm broken. I lean my head on Nonna's shoulder. She pats my back and whispers words of love.

I cry. I can't stop. A hole has opened in my world and I am falling. I have no parachute. I have no clever plan or witty repartee. I have loss and emptiness.

When I finish, Nonna takes my face in her hands and rubs a thumb along my temple.

'Keep your palm open, Bambino, if she is the other half of your soul as you say, then she'll return to you.'

I can't believe I have missed her by a couple of hours. I'd known in my spirit when she left London she was saying goodbye. I should have come straight after her.

Now it's too late. She must have driven away before it was even light because I arrived at Willows at six and she'd already gone. I hadn't been able to sleep and at one in the morning had made the rash decision to drive down.

I look across the room and out of the window. Oaks, ancient and thick, cluster on the other side of the drive. The early morning sun glistens off the dew on the leaves. They shimmer in the light. They are the green of Selene's eyes.

My soul stretches towards them. Come back to me my love, come back and make me whole.

Chapter 37

Selene – No More I Love You's

THE CABRIOLET SOFT-TOP IS BACK. My hair's tied back. As I drive I'm singing at full belt. Lung's wide, spirit soaring. Freedom fuels the power of the words as I sing along with Annie Lennox...

> *Do Be Do Be Do Do Do OH.*
> *No more I love you's*
> *The language is leaving me*
> *No more I love you's*
> *The language is leaving me in silence*
> *No more I love you's* (Annie Lennox 1986)

I've left Giovanni a letter at the cottage, trusting someone will pass it to him. Nothing like ink for letting the real you out into the open. Thank you, that's how I had started the Dear John.

Dear Giovanni

Thank you. My life would have been different if I hadn't met you, and although maybe in hindsight I should have stayed away from you and your come-to-bed eyes, I'm glad I didn't because you have changed my life by changing me.

I didn't know who I was when I first turned up in Cockington. I still don't, not fully. But I've come a long way. You have brought me to life in ways I never knew possible. You've made me feel things I thought were myths and only happened in movies (don't get big-headed, you're already a size XXL when it comes to confidence).

I'm sorry I'm writing this instead of saying it face-to-face, but I don't trust myself. If you asked me to stay it would be practically impossible to say no. So, I've taken the coward's way out and put pen to paper.

Before I allow myself to get swallowed up by another person, I need to find me. As you know, I'm on the path of discovery, and I'm excited about the future.

But I can't let myself be consumed by 'conforming' ever again.

I need to learn the art of saying no.

So, I chose me, not us. Because 'us' means everything you want, and because you come in a personality package I'm not overly keen on. Sorry to be brutal. But when I get married, I want to be with someone who gets me. And also someone who doesn't have his eye on every other skirt in town.

Take care of yourself my handsome, it's been fun!

The… 'one who got away,'

Selene xx

I was deliberately harsh. My reasoning is that you have to be cruel to be kind. By being blunt I hope I enable him to get over me quickly.

Blimey, but I love this song! I blast away with Annie...

No more I love you's
Changes are shifting outside the words

No more I love you's – well for a little while. Maybe when I get my head straight and stop drifting through life on the whims of others, maybe then I'll have enough space to allow love in… and the guts to say yes.

Epilogue

Giovanni – Two years later

THE CAMERAS CLICK AND FLASH, I smile. As much as I hate the paparazzi they're here to spread the word. My charity *Deep Pockets* is having its first major fundraiser. Thanks to the family's business I've been able to invite the crème de la crème of society. Film stars, politicians, even some royalty. When it comes to looking good in the public eye it's amazing how many celebs will make an appearance.

Deep Pockets is about the rich feeding the poor, not only in England but around the world. I'm not too sure how I managed to get it going really, but here we are – apparently – a huge success.

I shake hands with Mr. Sexy Voice himself, Tom. His grip is firm, his smile genuine. That he's come on board as charity 'champion' still gets me in the chest. He might have started off telling children's stories but he's come a long way, and I'm sure half the crowd has have come purely to get a glimpse of him. Great fellow, will always be in his debt.

The rich and beautiful saunter passed me on the red carpet on their way into the gala. A flicker of nerves makes my stomach cramp. It's going to be fine I tell myself, nothing to worry about.

After all the speeches and auctions I make my way through the myriad of tables, thanking people for coming and supporting the event. I'm sure my back must be bruised badly after the amounts of back pats-come-thumps I've received.

An unbelievable intake of air draws on a whisper, freezing me to the spot. Heart thuds, muscles tighten, sweat trickles, hands instantly clammy where just a breath before they'd been dry. The world tilts, I'm dizzy, my eyesight blurs… before slowing coming back into focus.

Two tables away from me is a group of people in a heated discussion. One woman is sitting back in her chair, watching and by the look in her eyes dissecting all that is being said. Her flaming-red hair is piled on her head in a soft swirl. She's slimmer than she was two years ago, and she looks… more sophisticated. Where has she been? What has she been doing? But more importantly, what is she doing here?

I don't know whether to approach or turn and run.

Fate. Timing, whatever you want to call it.

Her attention is pulled towards me. Our eyes lock. Will she smile or frown?

She does neither, she just looks.

Shit, but my heart is pounding. Two years I've been searching for her, and just when I'd given up ever finding her – here she is! Go figure!

Merda, she's standing up.

Should I turn away? Should I stay?

The room must have a thousand people in it, the orchestra is playing swing music, but I can't hear anything. The room has fallen into silence; outside of the image of her there is nothing.

She moves towards me. Confident strides. Her long legs knock against the deep-blue silk, which clings to her body and swirls around her feet.

She's a Goddess and she's smiling at me.

'Hi.'

I can't answer. My mouth is dry and there's a lump in my throat. I want to check out her hand and see if she wears a ring, but I can't take my eyes off her face.

'I guess you didn't know I was coming then.' Her eyes are sparkling, is she making fun of me?

'Can I buy you a drink?' Crap, that's my opening line?

'I hear it's an open bar?'

Awkward laugh, 'Yeah, that's right, but as I'm paying for it then I guess technically I'm buying, right?' My muscles are relaxing, tension slipping away. She's here, she's unbelievably here.

I offer my elbow, she hooks her arm under it, and I guide us to the Champagne lounge.

A waitress offers us a tray with flutes full of bubbly, I take two and we sit on a white lounger in the corner of the room – as far away from the rest of the world as I can take her. She might not stay long, and there's so much I have to say.

'Should I have known you were coming?' I go back to her earlier comment.

'I'm on the guest list.'

My heart pumps blood out so fast I feel like a hammer's just hit me in the chest. I didn't see her name; does that mean she's married? 'I didn't see it.' Maybe Kevin added it after my last glance over? I'll have to check.

'I'm with the Dorian Corporation, they paid for a table of eight, I thought they had to list the guests they were bringing.'

I breathe out slowly. In… out. Heartbeat slows. Get a grip man. I smile. 'Arr, that's why I didn't spot you, I checked out each table but only looked at the booking names. So are you still Selene Hastings?' I want to laugh at the outrageous question, but I can't. Right now, I'm nothing but deadly serious – and a nervous wreck.

She shakes her head.

I think I'm going to vomit, I'm too late, after all the searching she's married someone else after all. I look at her left hand. No ring. I look back up at her face.

'I decided to go back to my maiden name, Saltmarch.'

Relief makes me get even sicker. I'm on an emotional rollercoaster. Don't mess this up… don't mess this up… don't mess this up…

'Gio?'

I look up.

'Are you OK?'

Be a man for f**k's sake!

'I looked for you. After you left I mean… I looked everywhere. I didn't think to look for you under your maiden name.' Can't help the mix of desperation and condemnation that both fight for emphasis.

'I left you a note.'

'Oh, come on! I think I deserved more than that.'

Pink spots bloom on her lovely high cheekbones. I watch her take a deep breath. It causes her chest to rise and fall, those perfect breasts. Eyes up you idiot! I shoot my eyes back to hers. Heat flushes my cheeks.

'That's not who I am anymore!' I blurt.

She laughs, not at me, maybe because of me. There are those tinkling bells that I love so much. Oh, but I want to make her laugh, Lord let me have a chance to make her laugh, please.

'So who are you then, if you're not Playboy Gio anymore?'

'I've not been with anyone since you left.' Geez what the bloody hell is going on? Have I lost all thought to mouth filters?

Her pink deepens to a deep red, and just like that – I know that she's had someone else, maybe more than one?

'I've changed a lot in the last two years.'

'What have you changed?'

I take a drink to buy some time. I've done so much in the last two years but I don't want to pour it all out in one go. 'I have come a long way with the help of my councilor; I can even drop things on the floor now!'

Selene smiles, her eyes are sparkling. 'That's good.'

'As you are here, you might know I'm pouring my energy into this charity now, and I've finally let go of my control issues, well as much as I could.'

'I'm pleased for you.'

'Where did you go?'

She sips her Champagne, is she wondering how much to tell me? I hate that she's been with someone else. Maybe she's been in love? Still in love?

She puts the glass down and her focus pins me down. Eyes lock. Connection, oh sweet connection. I reach across the table. She draws back her hand and puts it on her lap. I sit back. Whatever happens, or doesn't happen, is up to her. That lesson has truly been embedded; she's a woman who wants to be in control of her own life.

'I've been to a few places in the last two years, but mostly Kenya.'

'Really?' No wonder I couldn't find her.

Leaning forward again, her adventures pour out. Kenya had been the first place she went, with a charity, helping to build a community school. The first trip had been six weeks long. But as soon as she got home she knew she had to go again. Now she works for *Oxfam*, very poor pay, but job satisfaction off the scale. In helping others, she's finally found herself.

'I'm so happy for you, Selene.' And I mean it. As she told me of her travels and the people she met, she came alive. Bubbles of life rising off her and filling the space between us, it made me want to forgive her for leaving without saying goodbye. In the hour it took to pour out her experiences I can no longer think of the past.

She's here now. And she's happy, and that's all that matters. I never stopped loving her, I still do. I ache to reach out and touch her, but I've finally learned to respect her boundaries.

Selene – Never Stopped Loving You

GIOVANNI IS MORE HANDSOME than I remembered. Tiny streaks of white tinge his hair giving him an edge of sophistication. His chocolate brown eyes are pools I want to dive into. He's changed, it's really obvious. I don't just mean the womanizing – I'd been following him these last two years in the press, reading everything I could find. Women have vanished from his life, except for his mother and sister of course. When going to functions it has been one or the other of them on his arm.

But it's more than the womanizing, that has changed. He seems calmer, more relaxed in his skin. I know he's longing to pull me into his arms, it's written all over his face. But he's holding back, the old Gio wouldn't have.

When I'd first driven away from Cockington I'd been sure I would be able to forget him. Not so. Memories of him flooded my dreams. When I was in the arms of a man, visions of Gio would float before me. I've had three flings in the last two years, and artfully dodged my way out of any commitment the moment they murmured three little words or started talking about the future.

I thought I did it to keep my identity, to be able to do as I please, but lying beneath everything I've done was the memory of my Italian lover. His smell, touch and moves, along with the lilt of his half-English half-Italian accent. His body on mine... the way he made me feel about myself. No, I'd never forgotten our summer romance. And that's why I'm here; when Shelley told me she had tickets for the gala I'd begged her to let me come without anyone knowing. I'm still not sure how she did it, that angel of mine, but here I am. She managed to slip me unnoticed onto a table of her old work colleagues. The other promise I extracted from her was that she wouldn't tell her husband that I was here. That she found harder. Just thinking of the happiness she's found with Francesco makes me smile.

Thanks to her loyalty, here I am.

Sitting opposite the man I love.

Wanting him more now than I've ever wanted anything in my life. Not just because he's changed, for if I'm honest I was heading back to him even if he was exactly the same person but because he's home.

He's where I belong, and having *found myself* I've realized I'm not whole unless I'm with him. Go figure!

'Did you really look for me all this time?'

'I did.'

'Why?'

'Because you are the life that fills my lungs, and without you I can't breathe.'

My eyes flood with tears that don't spill, instead they swim across my irises blurring my vision. When the lump in my throat fades I ask, 'But for two years?'

'If you asked me to stay it would be practically impossible to say no.'

'What?' I'm confused. I reach for a napkin and dab at my eyes, I'm having an emotional moment, however, this make-over at the beauticians cost me a fortune! Money well-spent by the way Gio is looking at me.

'That's what your letter said. That's how I knew I just had to find you, because once I had you in my arms you would say yes. It's what kept me going.'

'For two years.'

He smiles. 'For two *very long* years.'

'Gio…'

'Yep…'

'Please hold me.'

In a smooth swish, he slides across the white leather and engulfs me in his strong arms. Kisses rain down on my hair. My heart swells with gratitude. How lucky I am, to have found this man… again. The air around is like a sweet blanket, soft, smelling of honey.

'Amore mio.' With one finger he tilts my chin until I am only inches from his face. His warm breath touches my lips before he kisses me.

So cliché to say fireworks explode inside me, but what else so accurately describes the rush of joy, the sparks of life, the flutters and the rapid heartbeat?

Gio pulls apart by millimeters and whispers, 'And wilt thou weep when I am low? Sweet lady! Speak those words again: Yet if they grieve thee, say not so – I would not give that bosom pain.' (Lord Byron 1817)

'Byron,' I smile.

'You should see my poetry collection now, you're going to it. I've built us a house on the cliff looking out to sea. The library is a circular room with a huge window looking out over the beach. There's a bench that's practically a bed for you to curl up and read to your heart's content...'

He catches his breath and pulls back. Cupping my face in his hands he blinks and becomes solemn. 'Only if you want. I built it with you in my mind every step of the way, but if that's not what you want I'll sell it. We can live wherever you want.'

'Do you know what I want?'

'What?'

'For you to shut up and kiss me!'

His arms crush me; his lips demand my full attention.

I might have flown away for a while, but to his open palm I'm returned.

I'm home.

When we come up for air, I grab his face in my hands and look into his eyes.

'I fell in love with you during our holiday romance Gio, and I never stopped loving you.'

What point is life, but to love? To give and receive of oneself, to share, embrace, experience, to have fireworks every day.

Oh, how greedy am I… for fireworks every day!

Thank you so much for reading Selene's and Gio's story, I hope you enjoyed their summer romance. If you have time to pop a review onto Amazon I would really appreciate it, reader's words of encouragement mean the world to me.

Sincerely, Angelina Amoss

Printed in Great Britain
by Amazon

30655055R00145